DOCTOR C

C000183952

Philippa Croft had decided never to fall in
love with a doctor again, and in coming to
work in Canada she had left her shattered
dreams behind. But it seems she is fated to
be thrust into contact with yet another
member of the medical profession when
she meets her patient's attractive son,
Dr Harley De Winton.

Books you will enjoy
in our Doctor Nurse series

THE RETURN OF DR BORIS by Lisa Cooper
DOCTOR IN NEW GUINEA by Dana James
PARIS NURSE by Margaret Barker
ROSES FOR CHRISTMAS by Betty Neels
NURSE IN BERMUDA by Helen Upshall
YESTERDAY'S LOVE by Judith Worthy
NURSE BRYONY by Rhona Trezise
THE FAITHFUL FAILURE by Kate Norway
SURGEON ON SKORA by Lynne Collins
THE CRY OF THE SWAN by Sarah Franklin
NOT AGAIN, NURSE! by Leonie Craig
WESTHAMPTON ROYAL by Sheila Douglas
SURGEON'S CHOICE by Hazel Fisher
NURSE AT TWIN VALLEYS by Lilian Darcy
DOCTOR'S DIAGNOSIS by Grace Read
THE END OF THE RAINBOW by Betty Neels
A NAVAL ENGAGEMENT by Elspeth O'Brien
MATCHMAKER NURSE by Betty Beaty
STAFF NURSE ON GLANELLY WARD by Janet Ferguson
DR PILGRIM'S PROGRESS by Anne Vinton
A MODEL NURSE by Sarah Franklin
HEARTACHE IN HARLEY STREET by Sonia Deane
LOVE ME AGAIN by Alexandra Scott

DOCTOR ON THE NIGHT TRAIN

BY

ELIZABETH PETTY

MILLS & BOON LIMITED
London · Sydney · Toronto

First published in Great Britain 1984
by Mills & Boon Limited, 15–16 Brook's Mews,
London W1A 1DR

© Elizabeth Petty 1984

Australian copyright 1984
Philippine copyright 1984

ISBN 0 263 74687 9

All the characters in this book have no existence outside
the imagination of the Author, and have no relation
whatsoever to anyone bearing the same name or names.
They are not even distantly inspired by any individual
known or unknown to the Author, and all the incidents
are pure invention.

The text of this publication or any part thereof may
not be reproduced or transmitted in any form or by any
means, electronic or mechanical, including photo-
copying, recording, storage in an information retrieval
system, or otherwise, without the written permission
of the publisher.

This book is sold subject to the condition that it shall not,
by way of trade or otherwise, be lent, resold, hired out or
otherwise circulated without the prior consent of the
publisher in any form of binding or cover other than that
in which it is published and without a similar condition
including this condition being imposed on the subsequent
purchaser.

Set in 10 on 11½ pt Linotron Times
03–0584–54,560

Photoset by Rowland Phototypesetting Ltd
Bury St Edmunds, Suffolk
Made and printed in Great Britain by
Richard Clay (The Chaucer Press) Ltd
Bungay, Suffolk

CHAPTER ONE

PHILIPPA CROFT opened her eyes and looked down from the plane on to a changed scene from the hours of flying over ice floes with only the ribbons of deep blue sea threading between them. Now at last there was land in sight and a ripple of excitement ran through the aircraft as the passengers got their first glimpse of Canadian coast-line.

They flew on over black rocky wastes and lakes like tiny mirrors as they caught the sun's reflection. And then came the provinces of Manitoba and Saskatchewan and Alberta and below them lay Edmonton, like a beautiful city dropped from the sky into the prairie, as the plane circled around before coming in to land.

Rolling hills stretched away among lakes and rivers and green forests and, to the west, gentle uplands and majestic mountains. The North Saskatchewan River, snaking through the city centre of town, reminded her of the way the Thames found its way through London and out to the suburbs.

The airport buildings were a short way out of town, set among huge stretches of agricultural land and, as they touched down, Philippa realised how the time difference wreaked havoc with one's sleep pattern. She felt a little like a zombie as, carrying her hand luggage, she emerged into the building and followed the other passengers through numerous corridors to Immigration.

The excitement of seeing Emma and Oliver and her small nephew again returned. It had been suppressed during the long, almost nine-hour flight, and before that there had been the journey from her parents' home in Cornwall to Heathrow. Strange to think that it was already early morning at home.

The formalities over, she located her bags and passed effortlessly through Customs and suddenly, opening another door leading into the airport foyer, they were there to welcome her. Her sister dashed forward, unrestrainedly happy, grabbing her with both hands while Oliver followed, leading his rather overwhelmed son by the hand to greet his aunt from England whom he scarcely remembered.

Oliver was his usual thoughtful, positive self, taking her luggage and stowing it away in the boot of a king-size car parked at the kerb outside. He and Emma had met at a hotel management college and when they emerged with their various qualifications, she had married him and gone back to Canada with him. They now had a restaurant-motel on the outskirts of the city and were making money quite fast.

'How far is it?' Philippa asked when she could get a word in, while taking in the white ranch fences and trying to get used to being on the wrong side of the road, strange traffic signs and new territory.

'About half an hour . . .' Oliver told her.

'Isn't it rather cold? After all, it is May.' She had noticed they wore warm sweaters and suede jackets.

'Summer comes suddenly here, Phil,' Emma said. 'You'll see—any day now the temperature can go up to 70° or higher.'

'It feels a bit like snow at the moment,' her sister grimaced, shivering a little in her light suit. 'But I do like the crisp feel and the air seems so pure.'

'And being a nurse, you're all for clean air, I guess,' Oliver laughed over his shoulder as they sped along the highway. 'And we are up at quite a high altitude, you know. You'll soon get used to it. How was your flight?'

'Long and tedious most of the time—but then, amazingly spectacular in between. I think I enjoyed it immensely.'

'Good,' her sister gave her a discerning look. 'You've lost weight. Maybe this change of job is just what was needed. A bit drastic, but why not? I'm glad you decided to make a break—it means we see something of you. But wasn't it a coincidence that Edmonton was one of the hospitals on their list?'

'I didn't know that when I phoned London,' Philippa recalled. 'The paragraph in the recruitment section in my nursing magazine simply asked for SRNs for Canadian hospitals. Six month contracts offered and outward fare paid. It was done rather on the spur of the moment because I rang the BNA in London at once and had an interview within three days.'

'What did the parents have to say about your coming over here and giving up at St Andrew's after six years there?'

'They were a bit shaken, naturally. But I think they understood that I needed to get away. Dad did, I know. Mum thought it nice that I would see something of you. She did ask if it was what I really wanted. I said, no, it wasn't, but I thought it time to make a move and—here I am. I hope I'm not going to be a bother to you Emm—I can always get a flat if so—or there might even be a hostel for nursing staff.'

'Don't be silly. We're only too glad to have you, though you know that we have to be at the restaurant sometimes, don't you? You can always baby-sit this little guy here, if you've nothing else to do on your days off.'

They turned off the highway and into a drive-in where small chalet-type apartments surrounded a centre of trees; she saw the restaurant, long and attractive-looking, and a chalet house which Emma said was their home.

Inside, the décor was Scandinavian and good. The kitchen, with its wood fixtures and brass fittings, had everything to make it quite perfect.

'Heavens—it takes my breath away,' Philippa gasped. 'Just wait until Mum sees this . . .'

'They're always too busy to get away, or so they say. And what did you expect? That we still lived in wooden huts? No—it's mainly the one-nighters who do that, thank goodness.'

In her room, Philippa unpacked and bathed luxuriously. It was good to be here, she decided, although now she was feeling desperately tired and, after supper, made her excuses and went to bed early.

But as she lay there listening to the cars coming and going, catching a little of the music filtering through from the restaurant and, as darkness fell, the coloured lights casting a rainbow glow on the tree branches outside her window, she felt suddenly nostalgic for life as it was in that small Cornish village overlooked by the hospital.

She'd had no ambitions to leave it, especially after Nick came there as Casualty Officer, bringing with him the reputation of being something of a rake. But she hadn't believed it, even when after only a month he had taken her love life into his very experienced hands, broken through any reticence she still felt and taken her on to cloud nine with him. She'd had no doubts that it wouldn't last—forever, if need be, and for almost a year it had. Until Dr Moira West came to Obstetrics straight from university. After that the suffering had really begun. She had to get away. He had excused it with, 'Just one of those things, love. After all, we're adult— you must have known it could happen.' But she hadn't.

She had no alternative but to run away.

She slept fitfully after that and the next day Emma let her take the wheel of her red car to get used to the left-hand driving and discover her way about.

'You might find it a good idea to get yourself a car,' she suggested. 'It's quite a way to the hospital. In any case, you're doing very well. Just watch the signs. When do you actually start work?'

'On Monday morning. At seven-thirty. In at the deep end, as it were.'

'That means we have a couple of days to show you around. Get your bearings, I guess. It is lovely to have you here,' Emma said.

'It's—the best decision I've made lately,' her sister responded, for once in complete agreement.

The following day they drove out again to the shopping centre which was also something of an experience for Philippa, and again she drove their car.

'Aren't you scared I'm going to smash it up or something?' she asked her sister teasingly.

'No . . . You're a very good driver. I think you've got the hang of it very quickly. You could take Danny out tomorrow if you feel up to it. We've got a rather special lunch party and I have to be around. Normally we have a baby-sitter but she can only manage evenings this week. It looks like being a fine day, too.'

Danny was delighted when they all awoke to a sunny morning with skies blue and dazzling, though the air was still crisp.

'Where could we go, do you think?' Philippa quizzed her young nephew. 'Do you have any favourite places?'

'Oh, the lake, please . . .' he begged. 'Could we?'

'He's crazy about boats,' Oliver broke in, 'but I guess Storyland Zoo at Laurier Park or even the Game Farm where you'll see a buffalo herd is only a half-hour drive on Highway 14. On second thoughts—maybe Storyland is safer.'

'Oh—the lake, Daddy. It's not frozen over now.'

'I should hope not,' Philippa said laughingly. 'It's almost summertime.'

'It hasn't long been free of ice,' Emma remarked. 'We drove over it in a snow-mobile a few weeks back and Oliver even went ice fishing.'

'And I skated,' Danny put in. 'But the boats have started now. Could we go out in one—just you and me? Please?'

'Can you handle one?' Oliver asked her seriously.

'I live near the sea. Remember? It really is a lovely morning. What do you think?'

'Okay—I'll give you directions and there's a boat-house right by the landing stage beyond the parking lot. Danny's been there—he'll show you. It's only about fifteen minutes driving. But do remember you're driving left-hand—all the way; and watch the signs.'

'I'll be careful,' she promised.

With a picnic basket in the back and Danny safely strapped into his seat, she drove the car out of the drive and turned on to the highway. The lake was well sign-posted and when they arrived the sun was glinting on its blue waters. The tall trees around the shore were reflected in the rippling water. Already a few people in boats, brightly painted, were moving gently on its surface.

'It looks inviting, Danny. We'll take our basket out with us. I wonder how many miles long this lake is? I can't see the end of it yet.'

'It's kilometres,' he corrected her gravely.

'So it is. How silly of me.'

'Can we have a blue boat?'

'I expect so. We'll ask for a blue one, shall we?'

She was really enjoying being with her small entertaining nephew who stoically took the other handle of the picnic basket and waited to show the boatman which one he would like to go in.

While Philippa insisted on getting Danny into his yellow life-jacket, she didn't think it necessary to struggle into the one provided for herself, wanting to feel free. Pulling the starter cord of the outboard motor, they moved smoothly out and along the shore line, Danny dabbling one small hand in the water.

'It's freezing,' he said gleefully.

'Well—sit still or you'll be taking a very cold bath,' she warned. 'Do you swim?'

'Oh—yes. Not very far though and mostly in our swimming pool in the summer.'

'I see. Well, I imagine this lake is very deep.'

'Daddy says it is. I think it's going to rain soon,' he observed, looking up.

'Oh, no. The sun is beautiful. It's quite warm now.'

And it was very pleasant skimming through the ripples with the sun on their backs, although colder in the shade of the trees, so Philippa steered the boat away from the shore with no thought of turning back yet. She hadn't in fact realised how far behind them the boat-house was, and that they had rounded a jutting band of trees and now faced an expanse of water no longer broken with the coloured life-jackets of other people. In fact, it all looked rather lonely and sombre because of the grey rocks.

'I think we'll turn back,' she said brightly, 'and maybe it might be a better idea to have our lunch on the shore, Danny. You could be right about that rain . . .' as a spot hit her nose. Besides, the lake had gone a rather nasty shade of gun-metal grey and a gust of wind caught her hair, blowing it across her face and, at that moment, without any warning, the outboard motor spluttered and went silent and the small boat began to rock helplessly.

'Oh—no . . .' she groaned, making an unsuccessful attempt to start it up again.

'What shall we do?' Danny asked unhappily, sitting very still at the other end of the boat as he had been told.

'We shall just have to row,' his aunt replied cheerfully, with more conviction than she was feeling, as she reached for the oars lying on the floor of the boat and, slipping them in, began to turn with some difficulty, keeping a watchful eye on the small figure of her nephew in his yellow jacket, holding on to the side and being very quiet now.

The sun had disappeared behind some heavy clouds which came in over the hills without warning. A strong wind whipped the lake into waves of an ominous black. Danny began to cry when another gust of wind brought water into the boat and Philippa knew she must prevent him panicking at all costs.

'Sit very still, darling. Don't move. We'll soon be back.'

'I'm cold . . .'

She was too. Her thick sweater was letting the icy breeze through. Furthermore, it was difficult to keep a straight course. They seemed to be drifting towards the deeper parts of the lake and rowing to little avail. Danny was shivering now, as much with fright as chill, and as she reached towards him for a second, her oar slipped away.

He screamed then. Despairingly she looked for any sign of another boat but they had gone in when the storm first threatened. She couldn't even see the landing stage. Then she heard the hum of a motor and saw a boat skimming through the waves but the driving rain made it difficult to see properly and her hair stuck damply across her face as she waved hopefully.

A man wearing a red life-jacket was steering towards them, rain streaming down from his dark hair and glistening on his grim face. He looked irritatedly at her and at the small boy hanging on desperately.

'Thank God . . .' she breathed as he came alongside and held the boat, bringing it closer so that he could reach for Danny with the other hand.

'Give me the boy,' he demanded.

Lifting him bodily into his boat, he stretched out his hand for Philippa. Their wet hands clung together damply before he said angrily, 'Now—get yourself into that life-jacket.' He almost threw it at her. 'Of all the irresponsible stupidity—what the hell were you thinking of not to have it on?'

She was aware of the contempt in his face as well as his deep Canadian voice, as she fastened the straps with trembling fingers. As the boat shot forward, she lost her seat, feeling worse than ever. She was thankful that it was a bigger boat than theirs, which now drifted like a cork on the water.

Back on the seat she pulled Danny against her shoulder, sheltering him protectively. She was soaked to the skin. It was raining too much even to speak. Glancing surreptitiously at the man in control, his mouth still compressed as he looked towards the shore, nothing seemed important now, except immense gratitude towards him.

An anxious boatman stood waiting on the landing stage, reaching to tie them up. 'Storm came up fast, that's for sure,' he shouted. 'What happened out there and where's the other boat?'

'The engine stopped,' Philippa said briefly, after glancing at their rescuer; tall and rather commanding now that he was standing on the wood staging.

'The boat is okay,' he assured the other man. 'You can

go out for it later, I guess, but I would suggest you make sure engines don't fail in future.' He peeled off his life-jacket. He wore a brown shirt under a white chunky sweater. His brown pants clung damply to his lean figure. Philippa noticed these things subconsciously and then he had turned on his heel and walked with long, purposeful steps, up over the gravel to a low-slung sports car, parked next to theirs.

Taking Danny's hand, she hurried after him. He turned with some annoyance.

'What is it?'

'I—want to thank you,' she said in her lovely Cornish accent. 'I—can't let you go like that.'

His brown eyes flayed her as they met hers, corn-flower-blue, with no hint of subterfuge. 'Then perhaps the next time you will have more respect for the elements,' he said crisply. 'You must have seen that storm come in.'

'I didn't, I'm afraid. It came in so fast—I . . .'

But he turned on his heel after a flash of disbelief and slid into the driving seat of his car.

Still holding Danny's hand she unlocked the door of Emma's car, smarting from his words and tone, even while she had to accept the truth in them.

His car shot forward; the wind making his hair even more unruly. He threw her a brief, unsmiling glance, then was lost in a cloud of dust.

The rain had stopped as suddenly as it began and the sun coming from behind the clouds spread a golden sheen over the lake, changing its character completely. It was something she would have to get used to, this sudden weather pattern change.

'We've left the picnic basket in the boat,' Danny observed, watching her face. 'Do you think Mom will be mad at us?'

She nodded. 'Not only that—we could get it back if we phone later—but I think she might be with me for not taking more care of you.'

His parents were naturally very concerned when they heard the whole story, because she evaded nothing of the truth.

'Well—it is a bit early for that lake,' Emma admitted, 'and we should have warned you, when the wind gets round in that direction the storms can come in from the mountains so fast. But it seemed such a lovely day when you left. Perhaps—next time . . .'

Oliver was more direct, breaking in, 'Your sister needs to have more regard for the way things are over here. It's different from sleepy little Cornwall, you know. And next time—it had better be Storyland Valley. You can't come to much harm up there.'

'Oliver, I am sorry it happened. But we're both back safely and now we've had hot baths—there really is no harm done.'

'Thanks to the guy who rescued you. Who was he by the way? I'd better call him—you did find out?'

'No. He drove away too quickly and I very much doubt if he would have said . . .'

'Why?'

''Cos he was very mad at her,' Danny interposed from the sanctuary of an armchair in the corner, curled up in his warm dressing-gown. 'He made her put on her life-jacket, didn't he?' He looked at Philippa but she was looking at his father resignedly.

Oliver's eyebrows shot up. 'You mean—you weren't even wearing a jacket?'

She shook her head slowly, thinking gloomily that it was going to take some time before she rose in Oliver's estimation after this.

Later, in her room, as she checked her bag for the things she would need the following day at the hospital, she couldn't wait to get started there. Even though the first day might be difficult until she knew where everything was and met a few of the other nurses, she would at least be on her own professional level and retrieve some of her confidence in her own achievements after today's let-down.

She couldn't forget the brown eyes of her rescuer either. Nor his denunciation of her out of hand. How angry he had been. It might have been nice to meet him under different circumstances, she mused, knowing that now that was quite impossible.

Oliver drove her to the hospital early next morning, making no reference to yesterday's mishap.

When he stopped at the kerb outside the tall grey buildings, looking vastly different from her last hospital, he leaned across and opened the door. 'Will you be okay, now?'

She nodded, just a trifle apprehensively. 'I'll be fine, thanks.'

When she was out on the sidewalk, he bent his head to look up at her. 'It's going to be strange, you can expect that, but—good luck anyway.' He gave her a brotherly grin. 'Don't let it get to you—and as for yesterday—put it down to experience, Philippa.'

'Thanks.'

A hospital is a hospital all the world over, she told herself firmly as she went through the swing doors of the main entrance and saw the different departments on a layout map on the wall.

Crossing to the elevators, she went up to the top floor. An intern directed her to the room of the Principal Nursing Officer, giving her a second glance. People often looked twice at her. She wasn't beautiful, but her features were good and she had a clear, peaches and cream skin and never had eyes matched the cornflowers in the cottage gardens back home, as hers did. Her straight shoulders had a quality of grace—which was something special and naturally inborn—and her lovely head gave her a true Leo quality. She also possessed that kind of courage; as she knocked on the Chief's door she felt she needed it.

Her interview was short and soon over. A junior nurse was designated to take her to collect her uniform. A soft white cap, more substantial than those she had worn back home, now sat firmly on her pale gold hair; a white overall dress with short sleeves and white shoes completed her outfit.

Hanging her own clothes in the locker provided and deciding that her new image was a promising start to the new way of life she was trying to achieve, she followed the junior to her assigned floor and along more corridors to the quieter block which was for intensive care patients only.

'This is Sister Lasker's office,' she was told. 'If you'll just wait, I'll tell her you're here.'

So this was it. The start of her six months working in this hospital, she thought, when she was alone. The voluntary challenge she had given herself. The experience would be good if nothing else came of it. But just for a moment she wished herself back at St Andrew's where small was beautiful and she knew every bit of the building. No smooth elevators and not nearly so clinical as this streamlined hospital, she thought, gazing down at the unfamiliar white shoes and hoping that she had pinned her hair up securely and wishing now that Sister would soon appear before her latent nervousness became more positive.

Sister Lasker came briskly into the room, giving her a

quick, approving scan from the top of her head to her feet and obviously liking what she saw because she smiled. Afterwards, Philippa knew that she didn't do this too often, which was a pity because it made her rather square face into quite an attractive one. But she had hazel, rather bulging eyes, which seemed to pierce through one.

'So you're fresh out from the UK, Nurse Croft, isn't it? Thank heavens for someone with real experience behind them, even if you do have a rather fresh-out-of-class look. I'd better show you around while I have a free moment.'

'I'm to be here on this unit, Sister?'

She hadn't really expected to have so much responsibility until she had been there for a few weeks at least.

'Didn't anyone make that clear? You're trained in cardiovascular nursing, aren't you?'

'Yes, I am, Sister.'

'Right. Well, we've a patient, Mr Clyde De Winton, who has to be specialled and the nurse I had in mind has gone down with a virus. He came in yesterday morning with a myocardial infarction, but he seems to be holding his own. I don't want him to be left for a minute. I'll send someone in when you need to be relieved, or just ring the bell. There is an alert bell too on the screen, of course. Get yourself into his history notes. I'll just go through the report from night staff with you. He has been very unstable as one would expect but he seems to have straightened out. Now—I've asked for you to be put on this case because I don't want any slip ups,' she said crisply. 'He is by way of being a bit special. You understand that?' She gave Philippa a significant look which she failed to interpret. Was he royalty or something? And she could only monitor his progress correctly, after all, and give him trained nursing, with the benefit of experience.

'Now . . .' Sister Lasker went on. 'You're new here. So familiarise yourself with the layout of the floor as soon as possible and procedures, of course. I can give you a quick survey now, then I'll take you along to your patient in room four.'

Philippa followed her senior out into the corridor, her slight apprehensiveness disappearing in the environment she recognised. Stacked trolleys, chairs and medical stores; patients in rooms visible through glass partitions; an intern hurrying to a phone when his bleeper sounded; and two doctors on their way to a patient were assured that Sister would be with them in a moment. She was introduced to a nurse who would relieve her if necessary, cheered by her 'Hi . . .' as she put down her pile of clean towels and sheets to point out the clean linen room, asking, 'Do we call you Croft or Philippa?', obviously pleased at her 'Whatever you like.'

In room four Philippa saw at once that her patient, although pale and drawn, was still a good-looking man in his sixties. His thick greying hair denoted strength and his strong chin made up a face of obstinate character. She hoped fervently that he would make it. It was always sad to see a strong man suddenly weakened by illness beyond his control.

She read through his case notes in the file on her table, wondering afterwards what on earth could have been in her report from St Andrew's to merit this special responsibility. Her ears registered his breathing pattern for the room was quiet except for the bleep from the machine. She checked his physical freshness and made him more comfortable with the minimum of disturbance. She knew how much he would hate all this if he was aware of it but although he wasn't quite comatose, when she spoke his name quietly, he made no response.

That craggy face must be dear to someone she decided as she gently wiped the moisture from it, for he must have been virile and attractive to women in his younger days. Perhaps she would meet some of his family later.

A doctor came into the room then with an intern. She learned later that the former was a much respected cardiologist.

'Dr Barnes . . .' he said quietly, recognising that she didn't know who he was. 'I'd like the file, Nurse.'

He ran his eye down the pages and looked at the charts before going to the bed and checking his patient.

'More stable, wouldn't you agree?' He looked at the intern who was watching the screen.

'Yes, sir. His colour is improving too.'

The intern looked as pale as the patient, Philippa thought with some sympathy; knowing he had probably been up all night and was among the most overworked doctors in the hospital. That first year could be sheer hell when he was going through a dynamic period in his profession and experiencing how a good doctor is made. That intern year determined success or failure for him and this one looked as if he was just hanging on by his finger nails.

Dr Barnes discussed with them both his proposed medication change for his patient, writing it on the medication sheet.

'I'd like these started at once, Nurse.'

'Yes, sir.' Even though she had no idea where the dispensary was situated, she wasn't going to fall down on that. The intern must have read her thoughts for he picked up the prescription form with a sympathetic smile.

'I'll take this and get them sent up right away, Nurse.'

She smiled gratefully. 'Thanks.' The door closed behind them and she busied herself with making sure she knew where everything in the room was kept and could be reached at a moment's notice. Outside the sun had broken through and she opened the window a little, looking out over the rooftops and saw the tips of aspens bursting into scented green leaf below the window. There was a fresh breath of spring which gave her spirits a lift. She could pick up the threads of her life here in this hospital so far from St Andrew's with its painful memories and shattered dreams. Nick was still there. Did he think of her sometimes? Somehow it no longer mattered. He had no part in her new life and perhaps he had taught her something, even if it was never to let such a devastating thing happen to her again.

The machine warned of a slight fluctuation in her patient's condition as the current monitored his heart muscle, though there was no visible change and he stabilised, but she kept her fingers on his wrist, watching him intently and when the door opened quietly she didn't look round. The tablets, of course.

'Put them on the table. Thanks.'

The man standing behind her also watched the pattern on the screen readjust before his eyes came back to the nurse bending over the high bed. A shaft of sunlight rested fleetingly on her head, transforming the neatly-pinned blonde hair under the cap into a sheen of burnished gold. Philippa straightened up, feeling only the momentary warmth on her neck and saw him standing there regarding her with an uncertain expression. For her the recognition was instant. What was he doing here? Her instructions were, no visitors yet.

'I'm sorry,' she said softly, 'Mr De Winton is not allowed visitors. Are you family?'

His frown deepened. 'What are you doing here, when I gave explicit instructions for Nurse Sears to special my father?'

'I didn't know you were Mr De Winton's son. Nurse

Sears has gone down with a virus. I'm taking her place and it might be better if you came back later. He isn't responsive yet.'

'I have no intention of leaving,' he said icily. 'Neither do I need you here. Come back when I leave, will you?'

It sounded like an order which she had no intention of obeying, going to the door to receive the new medication from another nurse and bringing it to the table to check the instructions once more.

'I'm sorry,' she said, absorbed in writing on the record card. 'I can't do that.'

His head shot up then Calmly she met his eyes, knowing with a qualm of unease now that he had recognised her.

'I told you to leave, Nurse. I want to stay with my father for a bit.'

'Mr De Winton,' she said softly, 'I will not be ordered out of my patient's room when I have been instructed to stay. He is my responsibility and this machine needs constant monitoring, which you must know. He could have an arrest. Anything could happen. I can't leave. I won't.'

He reached for the charts at the end of the bed, turning the page deliberately before commanding her to, 'Ring the bell for Sister Lasker, Nurse, and say I would like a word with her. Tell her, Dr De Winton . . .'

Philippa's surprise at discovering who he was was masked with suppressed anger at the arrogant way he was behaving. Her cheeks burned. How dared he play with her in this cat and mouse way? He looked up from the notes. 'Or perhaps you would prefer to do as I requested in the first place.'

'No, Dr De Winton. I can't leave without Sister's permission,' she said quietly.

He pressed the bell himself and went to stand beside

the bed, looking down at his father, then silently concentrated his gaze on the tubes and wires before he too touched his wrist professionally.

Philippa felt dreadful. Nothing like this had ever happened to her before in the whole of her nursing career. She had felt it right to stand her ground, doing so without question and he should have understood this.

Sister Lasker, hastily summoned, had heard that he was here but she too was unprepared for his request as she glanced quickly at the bleeping machine as a certainty that nothing had changed as she said, 'Good morning, Dr De Winton. Is something wrong?'

'Perhaps, Sister, you will appreciate my natural wish to sit with my father for a while without this nurse breathing down my neck. She refuses to leave—obviously carrying her apparent conscientiousness to extremes. Is she new here?'

'Excuse me . . .'

Philippa closed the door quietly behind herself, refusing to stand by and be discussed as if she were absent. He had recognised her and was doing it deliberately—she was certain of that now.

Either his first impressions of her lack of responsibility from yesterday meant he didn't think her capable of looking after his father—or he wanted to bring it more forcibly home to her. Which was all rather childish—and not what she would have expected from a professional man.

She couldn't help overhearing Sister Lasker's remarks, 'Nurse Croft is just out from the UK, Dr De Winton, which is why I chose her to special your father.'

'So that's it.' He raised quizzical eyebrows which it was as well Philippa didn't see, but she might have felt better if she had heard Sister Lasker's personal recommendation of her a moment later.

CHAPTER TWO

AN AMBULANCE turned into the forecourt of the hospital below the window where Philippa stood gazing out at the rooftops, waiting for Sister Lasker. The patient was rushed into Emergency and even while she was still wondering if it was another coronary or whatever, more sirens wailed in the distance and soon more blue lights flashed on another hospital car and it too drew up at the entrance and yet another stretcher case was admitted. Perhaps that was where she should be; down there where all the action was. She could ask to be transferred, she supposed, to more generalised duties. Or even the children's section, which she enjoyed.

Behind her there was a panic on. She knew the sounds, the signs, and turning from the window saw the red light flashing and heard the alert bell sounding. An arrest. Automatically she hurried over to an oxygen tank, pushing it into the room behind a doctor who appeared and whom she hadn't seen before. A junior sister and another nurse rushed in then and she withdrew. She would only have been in the way.

But after three minutes' resuscitation she saw the doctor come out into the corridor, quietly speaking to an intern. She knew by the silence, the cessation of activity, that it was too late.

'Thanks anyway,' the doctor, passing her, said wearily. 'The oxygen. Quick thinking—just—no use.'

She didn't have to reply, neither did he expect one. She could see why they had needed as many qualified people as possible up here on this floor. So what now?

Would she join the team or be transferred elsewhere in the hospital, she wondered.

Sister Lasker went into her room, beckoning Philippa to follow.

'Do you still feel you did the right thing by refusing to leave, Nurse?'

'Yes, Sister,' she said truthfully. 'I didn't know that Mr De Winton's son was a surgeon.'

'Right. It was an exceptional situation. I think he should have told you; and been a little less demanding. However, he is part of the hierarchy and you know as well as I do that you don't argue with a surgeon. But you'll have to get used to him dropping in and out of the hospital. He's an orthopaedic surgeon at Prince George in BC. I believe he was down here for a seminar and his father came with him to see some friends. They were returning today.'

That, Philippa mused, would account for him being out on the lake yesterday. Alone.

'Go back now,' Sister ordered, 'and ask Nurse Robson to come to me. She's filling in for you. And remember, forewarned is forearmed, they say.' She allowed herself a slightly conspiratorial smile before sighing deeply as she said that there had been an arrest in room eight. 'They seem to have coped without me, but I must go along there now.'

I know—Philippa thought sadly, and it mustn't happen to Clyde De Winton. Not if she could help it. She was still speculating, when she reached his room, over the fact that his son was a surgeon. It explained a lot.

It was early evening and Clyde De Winton was restless. But checking his temperature and pulse rate she was relieved to find that the fever brought on by the necrosis of his coronary was abating slowly. It was a hopeful sign, always gratifying to note the downward trend of temperature on the chart and not an upward swing. His pulse, though, was still erratic and she stood looking down at him, her fingers on his wrist, calling his name, trying to rouse him a little, but he didn't respond totally.

Her back was to the door. Harley De Winton had come into the room without her knowledge, and stood quite still watching her, until he spoke,

'Nurse Croft. Will you come over here for a moment . . .'

His voice was low and controlled, different from that of the morning. She turned quickly. He was standing beside her table, tall and authoritative, the brown eyes under the dark eyebrows seriously speculative, while he waited.

'The fever is lessening, I see. And the breathing less shallow . . .'

'Yes.' She gave him the second chart at which he glanced briefly, then looked up, his eyes searching hers.

'I owe you an apology,' he said in a low voice. 'There is absolutely no excuse for the way I behaved this morning. You were quite right to obey instructions and refuse to leave your patient. It was also presumptuous to take for granted that you knew who I was.'

She met his eyes briefly. 'Thank you, Dr De Winton. I shall know in future.'

'I'd like to sit with him for a while but you will want to complete your report for the night staff, I expect.'

'I do have a little more to add to it,' she confirmed. 'Is there anything I can have sent up for you?'

He shook his head. 'I don't need anything, thanks.'

She was very conscious of him sitting beside his father, ostensibly reading the medical journal he had brought with him and certainly no longer interested in the nurse at the table; his apology made and already forgotten.

Then he stood up, looking down at his father discerningly as he touched his wrist before crossing the room and peering over her shoulder at the finished report. He ran his finger along under the result of one of the tests.

'Some arrhythmic there still,' he observed, as if she were a colleague, which did a lot for her self-confidence.

'Yes,' she said quietly. 'But it is very early to prejudge, isn't it?'

She felt she should call him 'sir', or at least something, but she couldn't just then because his hand, with spread fingers on the written page, touched hers as she reached for her pen and the brief contact sent a current of awareness through her body. He was much too close. She looked down at the onyx ring he wore on his little finger, at the fine dark hairs on the back of his hand and wrist, before he straightened up, taking with him the elusive scent of maleness and tangy aftershave.

She turned to respond to his curt 'Goodnight', watching his back view in the beige suit he wore as he brusquely left the room, not even closing the door.

His leaving had a steadying effect on her senses. He couldn't possibly have known what she had felt at his close proximity, surely? It would only have confirmed his initial opinion of her. Yet she knew now that he could be gentle, and that he was deeply concerned for his father.

But although Clyde de Winton made a slow improvement during the next few days, he was not out of the wood by any means. He had opened his eyes and looked up at her comprehendingly while she explained what had happened, then he had relaxed into sleep again; but later his son had enlarged a little more, warning him of the need to take his coronary seriously.

'I—feel better . . .' he said huskily. 'I like my pretty nurse. Where did you find her?'

'You are better,' his son assured him. 'You're getting the old twinkle back in your eye.'

Philippa, folding a towel at the wash basin, saw in the mirror above it that he had an amused quirk to his mouth as he spoke, but as he looked in her direction she hastily averted her eyes.

Clyde De Winton became quite possessive of his nurse after that, not liking her out of his sight for long, which meant that she was eating at odd times and leaving a little later, unless Harley was there. At night he was sedated so didn't protest too much then, but he became restless and excitable easily and refused to let anyone else wash or shave him and, except for the help of a male nurse, she did all the bed nursing herself. He was off the machine now, which made her job easier.

Each morning she was stoically driven to the hospital by either Oliver or Emma but she usually had to find her own way home at night, either by taking two buses or a yellow cab and she began to think seriously about getting a car of her own.

There had been storms overnight. But this morning the wind, blowing in from the mountains, was fresh and the air crisp in the early sunshine.

Emma breathed deeply. 'I love mornings like this,' she said to her sister. 'Just look at the sun reflected on the river down there. The traffic is good this morning. Of course, everyone starts work earlier over here than you do at home.'

'Except nurses—and doctors, of course.'

'Which reminds me—has your irate surgeon re-cognised you yet?'

'I'm sure he has. But he is no longer irate. In fact, he is rather nice . . .'

'But isn't it odd that he hasn't mentioned the lake episode?'

'He's keeping a strictly professional profile, Emm; and he does have other things on his mind. His father almost didn't make it and they're both away from home. Mr De Winton has a large ranch somewhere up there in BC. He's about to start itching to get back to it. And Dr De Winton to his patients, I imagine.'

'How do you feel now, Phil—about Nick and what happened back there? I've hesitated to probe but you seem to have coped pretty well. It must have been fairly shattering. Are you over it?'

Her sister thought for a moment. 'No . . .' she said, 'I think it did something to me which is going to take time. But all this helps. Nick . . .' her throat closed a little over his name, his image still too clear in her mind, 'is in the past now. I still miss what we had together, but it has lost something because it meant nothing to him—so—I . . .'

'Guess it's your ego that's still hurting,' her sister said cryptically. 'What you need is a new love affair.'

Philippa was glad that they had reached the hospital. She couldn't admit to it being an affair. It had been the first and deeply emotional love of her life and she couldn't envisage any other in comparison. But at least she was now able to talk about it. That must mean something.

A few minutes later Clyde De Winton's eyes were responding to her bright, 'Good morning.' He had been waiting for her to come for hours.

'Hi . . .' he muttered weakly. 'What day is it?'

'Thursday. How are you feeling?'

He grimaced. 'Not too good, I guess. I'll be better when I get out of here.'

She went to fetch his toilet things and fresh towels.

'Is Harley coming in soon?'

'He comes every morning.'

'I want to talk to him. About—going home . . .'

Adjusting his pillows she began to undo the buttons of his pyjama coat before she said gently, 'You need rest and to be stronger before you can make that journey. Dr Barnes explained to you, didn't he? You're doing so well; don't be impatient and undo it all.'

She saw his mouth compress stubbornly but he suffered her ministrations without further comment. Accustomed to making his own decisions, he hadn't become one of the wealthiest rancher businessmen in the province without taking a few chances. He knew that he could die at any moment. He was no fool. But frustration and being shut in these four walls was death to him. If he was going to throw in the sponge then he'd do it in his own ranch house among the pine trees in sight of the mountains. He wanted to get back near to his beloved Greta, buried under the grass within reach of the house, where he could go and talk to her whenever he felt like it. He had made up his mind. He wanted to go home. He hadn't the strength to argue; even this kind of thing exhausted him. For a strong man to accept his own weakness is almost tragic. Harley would know that he meant it—and know what to do.

'You . . .' he grunted, as Philippa supported him with her arm around his shoulders, while holding the glass for him to swallow his tablets, 'are the only good thing about this wretched business.'

Before she could reply there were steps in the corridor, the door opened and his son came in, his face breaking into a grin. He showed splendid white teeth when he smiled.

'Hullo there. You two look to be in a very compromising situation,' he observed teasingly. To Philippa his low Canadian drawl was fascinating, even though she was becoming used to his occasional light bantering remarks, mainly for his father's benefit. It was the repartee he enjoyed—when he was in good health.

He wasted no time now. 'Harley—I want to get home.'

'You aren't fit to travel yet, Dad. We'll go as soon as you are. You've been told to take things very slowly.'

Clyde glanced up at his son under bushy eyebrows. 'You can't stay here; what about the hospital?'

'Dad—that isn't your problem. I'm making a spring vacation of it—seeing a few friends.'

'Straight up—how am I doing?' Clyde asked huskily.

'Very well. Just don't have any setbacks. Worrying about the ranch won't help. You know it's in good hands. Brett can make any decisions that need making. I talk to him on the phone each evening and everything is okay. Relax, Father. Let someone else take the reins for a while.'

'You know I can't do that—never have done and won't start now,' his voice faded. His eyes closed and almost at once he drifted into sleep.

Harley sat looking at the craggy face before getting up and going to stand at the window while considering the situation.

'Nurse Croft.'

She came to stand beside him, her fresh skin with a kind of glow accentuating the cornflower blue eyes, slightly almond-shaped, one of the first things he had noticed about her; the second, her instant courage in the face of danger and the rebel in her which had amused him.

'I think . . .' he said deliberately, 'that we are going to have difficulty in persuading my father to stay here. But he needs hospitalisation for at least another month.'

'Yes. I agree.'

'He can't travel yet so we must just jolly him along for a bit, I guess. I'll need your co-operation . . .'

'Anything I can do, of course,' she said quietly in her soft Cornish brogue. Which, to the man standing looking down at her, was a departure from his usual way of distracting his mind from a problem.

'Just his special care nursing will be enough and pushing his confidence up—I guess. His medical advisors and myself will do the rest; thank you, Nurse.'

He turned and left the room, leaving her to ponder why her instant concurrence had sparked off a rather deflating return to his former arrogance. He really was the most self-opinionated man and not very easy to know.

Clyde de Winton, less sedated now, liked her to be around, talking when he could about himself. 'You understand, Nurse, that I'm like a fish out of water here in this bed—don't you?'

His son had just left after promising to go and talk to the chief doctor on his case, after yet another slight altercation.

'Yes . . .' she said honestly. 'I understand. And you aren't a very patient man, are you?'

'Never have been. I want something done before—not after.' He gave her a straight look. 'If I'm not going to make it—let them get me home where the last thing I see is my cattle grazing out there in the valley.'

She sat down beside him, impulsively taking hold of his hard, sunburnt hand with her slim fingers.

'But you are going to make it. Every day you are a little stronger. You've been lucky this time but it does mean you have to take life at a slower pace as Dr Barnes has told you.'

'Damn it—I can't do that. The thought of being an invalid scares me—I just couldn't live like that.'

'Calm down, Mr De Winton, or you'll be back where you started,' she spoke firmly.

'Okay. We'll see what Harley comes up with and take it from there.'

'Good. Now would you like me to read to you for a while?'

'Huh!—has it come to that,' he looked disgusted.

'Or try it yourself. The papers, or a magazine might take your mind off things.'

'No—too much hassle. You can read—if you like,' he said grudgingly.

She began the story of a French family who had trekked across Canada in the early days, finding it interesting enough to want to read on herself after she saw that he was dozing once more and had slipped into a deep sleep which was what she had hoped for.

That evening, out in the corridor, she called his son's name as he was leaving.

'Dr De Winton . . .'

He came back to stand looking at her quizzically, until she spoke.

'Your father is worried,' she said quietly. 'Mainly about his future potential, I think. He does need reassuring all the time.' She looked up at him, her head tilted to one side, the cap perched on her forehead as she always wore it.

'So that's it. I thought I had settled that point. You see, my father is normally the kind of man who doesn't discuss his worries with anyone—a private person. I wonder why he discussed them with you.'

'Patients often confide in their nurse as opposed to relatives,' she said flatly. 'It's still a question of privacy. Reticence about airing private feelings and fears with one's family. I just thought you should know.'

He said simply, 'There is a high degree of damage to his heart, I'm afraid. Dr Barnes has told me this today.'

'Yes,' she said in a low voice. 'I know.'

They seemed to be in some kind of unison then and her eyes clouded over slightly. 'It means a long convalescence, doesn't it?'

He nodded gravely. 'Even if there is no impediment or even relapse. But I think Dr Barnes is going to let him out of bed tomorrow for a short time to see how it goes. Goodnight, Nurse Croft.'

'Goodnight, Dr De Winton.'

He had almost turned the corner before she went into the room to wait for the night staff.

She was later leaving than usual, walking quickly towards the gates. She would get the eight p.m. bus with luck. But Dr De Winton's car slid up beside her and he inclined his head upwards as he leaned across to open the door.

'You obviously don't have a car?'

'No. I was getting the bus.'

'Not when I'm responsible for you being so late. Hop in.' She needed no second bidding. 'Where are we heading?'

Her face flushed as the scent of him reached her. So very personal, clean and sharp.

She gave him directions.

'Okay—we drive up the hill and around on to 107th Avenue. Then you can direct me.'

'Thanks . . .' she said gratefully.

'This is quite a city by night, isn't it?' he began then, as an apparent afterthought, he asked if she would like to go for a meal with him. 'Nothing spectacular,' he said, glancing at her pleated skirt and sweater. 'I know I'm springing it on you somewhat.'

'Oh—I can't, I'm afraid.' She looked crestfallen. She would have loved to go out with him.

'Sure?'

'I've promised to baby-sit my nephew.'

'Perhaps another time, then. I should have asked you earlier. I've wanted to all week.'

She threw him an incredulous glance, her hair, loosed from its restraining pins, fell over one eye in a golden frame, as she stared up at him.

'Really?'

'Don't look so surprised, even if you do look very seductive like that. I'm not entirely immune, you know. Must you go?'

She nodded affirmatively, completely off guard because of the stimulus his closeness brought to her senses. His long leg moved unwittingly against hers as they turned a corner. 'I promised . . .'

'And Danny will be waiting for you.'

She gave a small gasp. 'You've known all along, haven't you?'

'Most of the time. I just thought you'd prefer it this way. Besides—I wasn't very polite to you, was I?'

'I deserved it.'

'Oh—you admit that.' He flashed her a glance.

'I was a bit of a green-horn, but apart from the storm I didn't expect the motor to cut out like that,' she said soberly.

'And I couldn't bear the thought of you both drowning before I reached you. Hence the ribald language. It could have a psychological explanation. Relief—the way a mother feels when she slaps a child who has just escaped from being hurt, I guess. Although . . .' he smiled wickedly, 'you didn't inspire maternal feelings in me. Quite the reverse, in fact. I saw only a girl with cornflower blue eyes and wet, flaxen hair and a small boy

with freckles. It was about that time my father had his
coronary. When I got back to the hotel he had just been
taken to hospital.'

His teasing manner had changed. He looked serious
now.

'It's here,' she said quietly. 'The motel . . .'

'Oh—I didn't realise . . .'

He seemed surprised, then, 'I'll ask you again,
Philippa?'

'How did you know . . . ? My name?'

'I saw your signature on a receipt the other day—the
drugs.'

She was silent, then, 'I'd like that, very much.'

'Okay.' He grinned delightedly as she shut the car
door and began to walk into the house near the gate. He
watched her go but she didn't look back. It was almost
too unbelievable and her heart was beating very fast as
she went up to Danny's room, relieved to find him
already bathed and waiting in his dressing-gown for a
story.

Next day, as promised, Clyde De Winton was allowed
out of bed for fifteen minutes only. On the following day
for an hour. That evening it was decided that his son
could take him back to Prince George.

'Not the ranch, Father. Not yet,' he said very definitely. 'But you should be allowed home fairly soon, if
everything goes well.'

Clyde De Winton had to be content with that. It also
meant disappointment for Philippa because now there
would not be time for an evening with the surgeon.

'I have to get him out of here,' Harley told her. 'Both
Dr Barnes and I have been increasingly worried that he
will fret himself into another myocardial infarct if something positive isn't implemented; so we are taking the
risk of moving him.'

'How is he going?'

'By air ambulance. I shall travel with him.' He put a hand on her shoulder. 'I'm afraid it means our date has not materialised. I'm—sorry about that. But I don't have a choice. Perhaps the next time I'm down here—if you're free.'

'I'd like that,' she said quietly—so that he couldn't hear the tremor in her voice. It was terribly disappointing but, as he said, inevitable.

Next morning they left after the briefest of goodbyes, a hospital stretcher car taking them to the industrial airport where the air ambulance was waiting. As it was not very far, in twenty minutes they had taken off and were on their way up over the forests and lakes and mountains; one long step nearer to going home to the ranch he loved, which was why Clyde De Winton withstood the hazardous journey better than anyone expected him to.

He had clasped Philippa's hand as he left—emotionally; but he hadn't said a word. But he had left her a present. A lovely little fob watch for her dress. It was silver, set in pale blue enamel. Her own had come unpinned a day or two previously and dropped into the washbasin. He had known about that but she had no idea who had bought this beautiful replacement. The small 'thank you' card hadn't been identifiable either but she thought it just could have been Harley De Winton's writing. His father's was still too spidery to be recognisable.

She felt bereft after they had gone. She missed Harley's step in the corridor although that same afternoon another patient occupied the bed and a whole new set of charts and progress sheets were in the file on the table. Doctors came and went and she was now given the three patients on that corridor for her special care.

Although none of them needed the same degree of supervision as Clyde De Winton, there were other nursing qualities which were needed. And the day after tomorrow they would all be post-operative.

Tonight, she thought wanly, was her first early evening and probably when Harley De Winton would have taken her out for dinner somewhere. Her mood wasn't helped by Oliver, as she curled up on the settee with a magazine while Danny got a game set up which he hoped she would play with him later.

'Have your celebrities gone then?'

'Yes. They flew back this morning. So that's the end of that, I suppose.'

He shot her a second glance, hearing real regret in her voice.

'You got to like him, didn't you?' he said teasingly. 'Emma said that he had asked you out . . .'

'He did. But he left before we could go.'

'What is it about doctors?' he asked teasingly. 'We all know that the nurses fall for them—is it the glamour or part of the perks . . . ? Damn—I'm sorry, Philippa.' He remembered, too late, about Nick and now he got up and threw an arm around her shoulders. 'That was thoughtless and damned stupid of me.'

'And not very accurate,' she retorted. 'I think I'll get an early night.'

In her room she shrugged off her strange mood; sitting down to write to her parents and remembering that Nick was still there quite close to the hotel on the cliffs. Did he think of her sometimes? Was his affair with Dr West still on?

Why had she come so far to forget him when she was raking up the old memories? And if she was honest, wouldn't she admit to there being another man's face more constantly before her now? With brown eyes instead of green, and dark hair—not fair like Nick? She wished she knew how her patient had settled in. Usually, in a busy hospital, too many passed through one's hands fleetingly—here today and then when one came back on duty, another head lay on that pillow. A nurse got used to it—like everything else—but he had been her own special responsibility. They had talked together—he had waited for her anxiously each morning. She missed him. She missed them both, which was fatal.

Sister Lasker confirmed next day that Dr De Winton had called Dr Barnes and said that his father was resting after the journey which he had managed very well. 'I thought you would like to know that.'

'Thank you, Sister. I was a bit apprehensive that it might be too much for him.'

'I guess we all were. He still needs a lot of care but we did our best while he was here. I can't see him ever conditioning himself to being a semi-invalid though,' she mused. 'Much too strong a character.'

Philippa shook her head. 'That's the sad part about it; he must have been a very positive type of man previously.'

'He still is. By the way—there came a glowing report of you, Staff Nurse.'

'Oh . . .'

If Sister Lasker noticed the fierce blush which suffused her face, she made no comment. She hadn't been unaware that Dr De Winton seemed unusually interested in his father's special nurse. And after the way he had behaved on that first day it was even more noticeable when she saw Philippa actually get into his car one evening.

During the following week, Oliver and Emma took her sightseeing whenever they could spare the time, and she worked hard during her duty times at the hospital and got to know quite a few of the staff. She was accepted, already involved with new patients with varying degrees of risk care.

Until she was called to Sister's office just before lunch.

'You are wanted on the phone, Staff Nurse,' she was told briefly and she only had time to wonder vaguely why Sister Lasker had given her such a disapproving glare, when she heard a voice she had never expected to hear again, say, in answer to her quiet, 'Nurse Croft here . . .'

'Hullo, there. Dr De Winton. Would you consider the possibility of coming up here to Prince George? My father is making no progress—in fact he's being extremely unco-operative and is on his way to another attack if he doesn't cool it. He wants you to take over again. To placate him I promised to call you direct and try to persuade you. How do you feel about it?'

CHAPTER THREE

PHILIPPA needed some time in which to recover; time to think about his request, but he was asking for an immediate decision and while his words ran through her brain like quicksilver, the words came tumbling out with scarcely a tremor in her voice. 'Of course I will come, Dr De Winton, if you think I can be released that easily.'

'Good. I shall have to pull a few strings, but as it will probably be on a temporary basis it might be arranged. Right, Nurse Croft, I'll get on to it right away and get back to you later. And my thanks—for myself and my father. Now—will you have this call transferred to the Principal Nursing Officer and we'll see what can be done?'

She got through to the switchboard and made the connection, replacing the receiver gently when she heard his deeply authoritative voice speaking to Administration.

It was as well, she thought hazily, that he was not aware of her own accelerated heartbeats. What now? Would they release her? If so—she was committed. She hadn't hesitated, but how could she refuse when he put it like that, even if she had wanted to, which she hadn't. She was honest with herself in admitting that. To be at the same hospital with Harley De Winton had a very strong pull.

It would mean leaving Edmonton and her family though, but only for a time, until Clyde De Winton was well enough to go home to his ranch. After all, she wasn't over here on holiday but to work. After her six

41

months were up she would be able to afford to have a holiday because of the higher salary involved if she was specialling a patient.

As she went back to the room where Nurse Kelly was relieving her, Sister Lasker was speaking on the phone in her office and beckoned her in.

'You'd better go to lunch now, Staff Nurse—see me when you return.'

Then she continued her conversation but Philippa caught the disapproving look on her face and guessed to whom she was talking. She felt in a rather mixed frame of mind as she joined the other nurses in the elevator also on their way to the cafeteria.

The buzz of conversation hit her as she went in, but she was too absorbed in her own thoughts and let it pass over her head as she carried her tray to a side table, not noticing who sat opposite her. Should she have asked Sister Lasker's permission before she decided to go? she wondered. And what would be the outcome of that long-distance call which had thrown her into a deeply thoughtful mood?

The intern opposite grinned across at her over his spaghetti bolognaise and chuckled, 'Hi there. Are you just not with us or do you prefer not to talk while you're eating?'

'I'm sorry,' she smiled across the table, recognising him as being the one who had helped her out over the prescription. 'I didn't mean to be rude. I just have something on my mind.'

'Haven't we all? Eight hours' unbroken sleep—for my priority. I only had two hours again last night.'

'You're doing your first-year resident aren't you? That's not very enviable.'

'The most scary one of all the others, I guess. I'm surprised any doctor ever survives his internship year.

When it's a twenty-four hour stretch, lack of sleep is the worst hazard. That and making mistakes—the good things too, of course, like finding something that someone else has missed.'

'I know it's conflicting,' she said thoughtfully, 'because you have to delve into everything—obstetrics, surgery, medicine and paediatrics, all in one year, don't you?'

He leaned across the table, speaking softly, 'It's the year of the great divide, that's for sure. You make mistakes which scare you to death and learn more about your own limitations than ever before. I'm doing my stint on medicine right now and it's fascinating, but tough going; the pressure gets to be impossible, but you push on. Fortunately I do have a good resident in Dr Carne, which is my survival spot.' He looked hopefully into her blue, sympathetic eyes. 'I guess you wouldn't come out with me on Saturday and help me blow my top, would you?'

She shook her head slowly, 'Sorry . . .'

His pocket alarm bleeped then. He got up, throwing her a wry smile. 'I guess that's for me—see you around.'

But she didn't see him again, as it happened, because she was not around either.

Sister Lasker imparted the news of her transfer when she reported to her office.

'I'm not over the moon about this as you can imagine,' she said dourly, 'but not entirely surprised either. You've been given a temporary transfer to the hospital at Prince George, Nurse. You collect your tickets and timetable tomorrow morning at ten o'clock as the travel arrangements are being made for you from the other end.' She stood up. 'Goodbye then, Nurse Croft; and I hope we shall see you back here again soon.'

'Thank you, Sister. I hope so too.'

'You had better go off duty now. You must have things to do—packing or shopping.'

'Yes—packing,' Philippa said, feeling slightly bemused at the speedy way things were done over here. She half expected another call from Dr De Winton but none was forthcoming by the time she was ready to leave with all the necessary details she needed to know safely in her bag. And the yellow cab she had ordered was already in the hospital forecourt.

The river looked grey today; and the skies leaden as they passed over the bridge, teeming with traffic in both directions. This, she decided, was a city of movement, excitingly new; the buildings looking as if they had erupted from the prairies overnight. It was fast becoming a green and gold city as the trees began to burst open in the parks. A city waking up after the long, cold winter. There was still so much there hadn't been time to see and do here but she would be back. It was all so much larger than life as she knew it and just now she felt that she too was being swept along like the river below on a tide of new experiences, taking her off on a new tangent—north to Prince George.

When she reached the motel her news was received with some restraint. And Danny even gave a howl of protest.

Emma said guardedly, 'You didn't have to accept—did you?'

'No—but . . .'

'It's a long way, Phil—and not like it is here. Besides—you don't know anyone up there. When do you have to leave?'

She answered hesitantly, 'I'm not sure. Tomorrow morning I have to collect my tickets but I suppose I had better be ready almost at once.'

'You will get on the afternoon train,' Oliver told her.

'That is, if they want you up there fairly quickly. The trans-continental comes through here only two or three times a week and you'll have to change at Jasper in the Rockies to the overnight train to Prince George. I think it arrives there around seven-thirty next morning.'

'Next morning? Oh—it's as far as that then.' She was silent, for a moment, a little subdued now also.

'You should go out on to that little platform at the back of the train after you leave Jasper, depending on the weather, of course; but if it's a good night the mountains towering above will be a sight you'll never forget. Mount Robson is the highest peak in the Canadian Rocky Mountains, over twelve thousand feet.'

'I don't expect I shall be able to sleep on the train,' she observed.

He chuckled. 'If you like being rocked to sleep you might.'

She didn't dare to ask what he meant by that, getting the feeling that she was being teased; and it wasn't helping very much.

'You'd better strap Emma's snow-shoes on to your luggage,' he went on, but more seriously now. 'You might need them. In the paper tonight they report snow a foot deep up there.'

'Oliver—is that true?'

'See for yourself.' He handed her the newspaper. It was true—in black and white. People were still wearing fur hoods and some even snow-shoes in Prince George.

She grimaced. 'Well—I can't back out now,' she said resignedly. 'I've promised and the snow can't last for ever,' she added philosophically. 'Besides—I like snow.'

'Well,' Emma said quietly, 'if you have any problems, call us. And if things don't work out you can always come back here.'

'Thanks, Emm. But it isn't the North Pole. I shall soon get to know the other nurses and personnel at the hospital and—I'm not exactly a child, you know.'

'We know,' her brother-in-law laughed, shaking his head. 'But all the same, you just might get to feel quite lonely up there. And . . .' he advised, 'I should get an early night. You won't get much sleep tomorrow night.'

Philippa flashed him a grateful glance. He was being realistic, she knew, but as it happened he was proved right although not in quite the way he or Philippa envisaged.

The full import hit her next morning when she collected her tickets and rail times, discovering that she was indeed booked on the night train to Prince George as Oliver had predicted and the four-thirty from Edmonton that afternoon, and she still had to finish her packing.

Emma pushed in two warm sweaters of her own, 'And you'll need a warmer jacket than that raincoat,' she said practically. 'Take this one with a fleecy lining.'

'But I've got my cloak, Emma . . .'

'So—you aren't travelling in uniform, are you? Slacks and a sweater would be more sensible.'

'I was going to wear my blue suit . . .' She thought for a moment. 'Oliver was joking about the snow-shoes, wasn't he? They look like elongated tennis-rackets.'

Emma shook her head laughingly, 'I don't think you're going to need those. But it can snow up there until the end of May sometimes. Heaven knows what the parents will think about you taking off like this. I suppose you're leaving it to me to phone them?'

'Oh—would you? I'll write to them as soon as I get organised.'

'Okay. Now—have you got everything?'

'I—think so.'

In spite of an outward show of independence, she

knew she was going to miss them; and a slight nervousness attacked her as she strapped up her luggage and said goodbye later before following Oliver out to the car as he was to drive her to the station.

The terminal was alive with people and buzzing conversation in several languages, all awaiting the arrival of the trans-continental express which had already covered two thousand miles of Canadian territory.

She joined the queue waiting to go through the barrier, saying goodbye now to Oliver also.

'Take care,' he said briefly, thrusting some magazines into her hands. Then surprisingly gave her a quick kiss, murmuring, 'Philippa, you're crazy to do this . . .'

'I know,' she replied happily, at which he raised his eyes to heaven and left her standing there among people who spoke German and Polish, and American-Canadian, of course. She was the one who felt herself to be alien and already lonely. The train came in and stopped with a screeching of brakes and then she was going with them, up past the redcap who scrutinised her tickets and along the corridors to find her seat.

It was interesting after that, watching the other passengers loading, mainly bound for Prince George or Prince Rupert, and others, the student types, going on through to Vancouver, laden with guitars or their packs on their backs denoting that they were prepared to camp their vacation through. It was all food for thought and she found herself doing just that as the train started off over sometimes flooded tracks, towards the foothills.

The rivers were swollen with the melting snow rushing down from the hills. It became a little frightening as it laboured over bridges with waters swirling beneath at ten miles an hour. 'A red warning,' someone informed her casually. But as her informant was Polish and spoke little English the conversation was not continued.

The skies darkened to violet streaks and rain sleeted down the windows so that it was no longer possible to see anything. Then, as suddenly as on the day on the lake, it stopped; the skies were a vivid blue with orange and gold slashes of colour spreading away to the west. It would, she decided, be a glorious sunset tonight. But it was very cold, even though the windows were double glazed. She was amazed to find herself feeling a little homesick, which wasn't at all part of the sophisticated image she was planning.

Three hours later the train stopped at Edson, a sparsely populated town of pipelines and farming, and then it was time for dinner. This was a disappointment as it was impossible to eat properly because of the swaying of the train and sudden stops because of more flooding on the track. This, she decided, was a somewhat hazardous journey, and afterwards, snow appeared. On the hills mainly, but as they neared Jasper, after crossing the Snake River, and the mountains came into view, snow was very much part of the scene. In fact, as she peered through the windows of her carriage it became impossible to see where the peaks ended and the sky began. Besides, it was almost dark now.

She was very conscious of travelling alone. She missed the community feeling she had taken for granted back in Cornwall. Then, of course, Nick came into her reflections with no warning so that she could feel grateful that the ache in her throat no longer came when she thought of him. And the pain no longer jabbed at her consciousness. She had learned to live without him—he had been left behind in England. But did she have to come six thousand miles to do it? she wondered, as she gazed up at the massive peaks ahead of the crawling train. How unfriendly they looked, those mountains in the late evening dusk, especially Mount Robson—the highest of them all. But then this was Canada at its most spectacular.

And Dr De Winton—he had known she must make this long journey to Prince George. Surely there was another nurse on the spot to whom his father could adjust. So—why hadn't she simply said she didn't want to come?

Could it be that she was looking forward to seeing him again? Was it wholly because of her patient? Was it just the spirit of adventure, dormant in every person; or a chance to see Harley De Winton again? Maybe work with him; knowing how delighted he was at her assurance that she would take over the care of the older man and relieve him to attend to his own patients; his own life.

The train was slowing to a stop with a great deal of groaning brakes and she saw that the track ran along by the main street and the station. Jasper. Everywhere there were coloured lights. Up in the hills chalet houses glowed in the darkness while behind them loomed the mountains, shining with polished snow. Traffic moved along the highway, and across the street shops and restaurants glowed welcomingly in the darkness.

'The train for Prince George leaves in an hour from this platform,' her redcap advised her as she stepped down to the chill damp of an early summer night. 'Your luggage will be loaded on to it for you. The waiting-room is over there.'

An hour. Glancing round the waiting-room which was built like a huge log cabin, sitting on a long bench-type seat, Philippa listened while the other passengers around her conversed in either Polish or German with only a smattering of Canadian and there were also several Indian families with bundles and straw carriers waiting too.

Glancing at her watch, she decided to go across the street to Whistlers Restaurant, obviously because it was at the foot of Whistlers Mountain. So called, she discovered later, because at its summit lives the elusive Whistling Marmot.

The coffee was excellent. Black and strong as she liked it and it did a great deal to restore her flagging spirits, so that after she left to go back across the street to the station, she no longer felt the need to talk to someone. She enjoyed just gazing up at the huge mountain peaks all around the tiny town in the largest National Park in Canada—almost 4,200 square miles of it, Emma had told her. It certainly cut one down to size, the grandeur of those peaks towering above.

An errant moon slipped in and out of the clouds, the night sky blue-black in contrast to the white glistening peaks as she stepped back on to the station platform, grateful for the extra warm jacket her sister's forethought had provided her with, for it was icily cold.

She was debating whether to go back inside the crowded waiting-room when the train appeared, slowly sidling alongside. She decided to stay where she was until boarding time, hoping that her luggage was among that huge pile at the end of the station.

Turning up the collar of her jacket she looked up again at the glittering heights of the massive mountains, the moonlight catching her shining gold hair in its beam. And that was how Harley De Winton discovered her as he walked briskly from the car which had brought him the three miles from his patient, who was staying in one of the luxury cottages on the shores of Lac Beauvent near the famous Jasper Park Lodge—the jewel of the Canadian Rockies.

He stood for a moment watching her as she stood quite still, drinking in the beauty and grandeur of the night. It had been a stroke of luck that he was able to make the train, even more getting himself a couchette on it. It would have meant flying back to Prince George if he had missed it, because he had been away long enough.

His voice broke into her thoughts just as she began to move forward with the other passengers about to board the train.

Almost confidentially, he said in her ear, 'Hullo there. I'm very relieved to see you've made it this far without mishap.' And the laughter she heard in his voice had reached his eyes when she turned to look up at him in amazement, stumbling over his name.

'Dr De Winton—how on earth do you happen to be here when I . . . ?'

'I know—you thought I should be at Prince George. I do travel around, you know. This was an emergency. I'll tell you about it later—but right now—we had better climb aboard.'

She found herself walking beside him, propelled sometimes by his hand under her elbow to the last coaches where their couchettes were situated. Climbing aboard was an apt description; the redcap had placed steps for them to reach the carriage, and he scrutinised their tickets and directed them. The surgeon's cabin number was next to hers. She didn't let him see that this was another pleasant surprise and her uncertainties about the rest of her journey were disappearing fast. She might even enjoy it, she thought happily, as she put down her overnight bag and inspected her very compact cabin.

It was very noisy outside and she was wondering if it was worth the trouble of undressing and getting into the beautifully made bed, with its snowy sheets, as she let it down from the wall, when someone tapped on the door.

He saw the bed was down and that she had removed her thick jacket.

'I don't think you'll get much sleep for a while,' he said complacently. 'How about a drink—or coffee?'

'Won't the corridors be rather too crowded to get through to the dining-car?' She knew that most of the passengers had settled for just a seat for the night.

'I have both in my room.'

'Oh—then perhaps coffee . . .'

He stood back, closing her door after her and bringing her key, dangling it from his finger before dropping it into her lap as she sat down on his settee.

The train may not leave until midnight even,' he said easily. 'Going to bed yet is just a waste of time. Besides, I'd like to talk to you.'

'I—haven't asked about Mr De Winton yet,' she said remorsefully. 'He is still at the hospital?'

'Yes. I just hope your coming will stabilise him.'

'There are more complications then?'

'I'm afraid so. The damage is rather more extensive than we thought; his heart is in poor shape. He has probably been having warnings for some time which he ignored although I've repeatedly stressed that he should not disregard any specific changes. Which is one of the reasons I persuaded him to come away for a few days with me. He has friends in Edmonton. I guess I was too late. But as you know already, no one tells my father what he should or should not do. Cattle ranching is his whole world; he has always had his finger on the pulse of his business deals and the day-to-day running of the ranch, making his own plans and implementing them. Well . . .' He took a deep breath before going on, his expression serious. 'Now he is going to have to delegate most of it to my adopted brother, Brett, who is perfectly capable of running it. Father must give way. In fact, his whole life-style is going to have to change very considerably. Whether or not he will accept it when he has an assessment in a few days, I don't know.' He put down his cup, meeting her eyes frankly. 'A build up of frustration could precipitate another, possibly fatal, attack. I need your help. You seem to be the only one he wants around him while he is immobile. It's all a little out of context, of course.'

'Your own work has some priority too,' she reminded him gently.

He nodded. 'I've a backlog. My list grows daily but I can cope with that. Having to fly down to Jasper to a friend in some distress is just a part of it. I've immobilised him for three weeks before I make the decision whether or not to do a laminectomy and fusion on his lower spine. This time, I think I must.'

'Does he have a history of disc troubles then?' She was interested in orthopaedic surgery, having done a lot of theatre duty in this particular field.

'Over the past few years, yes. But,' he went on resignedly, 'because he had been okay recently he had ventured on the ski slopes and came a cropper. But— back to why you are coming up to Prince George. Frankly—we do need you. I hope you won't regret your decision to come up into the backwoods.'

'I don't think so,' she told him quietly as the train jerked and began to move noisily along the track.

She stood up then, a little shy of his rather close proximity in the tiny available space, the train's sudden jerking throwing her against him, to be quickly steadied by his hand on her arm.

'You'll get used to it,' he grinned, 'by the time we reach Prince George. There is worse to come.'

'Thank you for warning me. I think I had better get back to my room. Goodnight, Dr De Winton.'

'Goodnight.'

He watched her unlock her door, then went in and closed his. She pulled her blind aside and tried to look out but they seemed to be climbing up through a mountain. She could see only grey rock. It was very hot and stuffy now, the fan above the door seemed to have stopped functioning for some reason, and she no longer felt like going to bed.

She tried to interest herself in a magazine, glancing through it at the gay summer fashions. Sophisticated clothes she would like to possess but either could not afford or hadn't the social opportunity to wear them.

The train literally rocked its way along the track, going very slowly as if it knew the hazards. There seemed very little air. She washed her face and brushed her hair but still didn't undress because she had remembered what Oliver had said about the open air platform at the back.

She reached for her coat and, locking the door behind her, went along the silent corridor to the door at the end. It was exactly as in the western films she had seen on television.

But someone else was already there.

'I'm glad you came . . .' Harley De Winton said softly. 'Share this ethereal spectacle with me, won't you? You may never have this opportunity again. Shame to miss it.'

He had seen her hesitation and hoped she wouldn't go.

She didn't know how arresting she looked, her face caught in the silvery light as the train emerged and they looked back to where Mount Robson's snowcapped peaks towered above them into the night sky and the huge moon up there in the velvety darkness seemed to shine just for the two people on the back end of a train. It all seemed unreal and the man close to her shoulder even more so as he explained the grandeur, naming each mountain, while the train lurched precariously, necessitating holding on to the handrail or one of them could easily be pitched off.

'It's awe-inspiring, isn't it?' she breathed. 'Hard to take in such large doses. A bit frightening too, unless one is used to it,' she confessed.

'Yes. I suppose it does have that effect, especially after your minuscule part of the world, Philippa.'

He said her name quite naturally. It made her heart plunge as she sought for a quick retort. 'England isn't all that small. Have you ever been there?'

'Strangely, no. Europe is something I've been promising myself in the near future.

She shivered as a blast of freezing air came through one of the gulleys in the rock. 'I'm going back now,' she murmured.

'You're cold.' His hand turned up the collar of her jacket, coming to rest against her cheek. She wondered if he felt her tremble at his touch as he looked down at her, his eyes unreadable in the moonlight, as she turned abruptly towards the door.

It was he who opened it for her and they passed through silently into the corridor, separating at their respective doors.

'Goodnight.' His voice was almost a whisper, so as not to waken other passengers, but she didn't answer, closing her door quickly to stand with her back against it, touching her cheek where his fingers had been a moment ago, leaving a warm glow somewhere in her body.

This, she decided, as she slipped into her housecoat, was the last thing she wanted. Another involvement with a doctor and a consultant at that. It mustn't happen. No matter how lonely she may feel; no man was going to bring a return of the devastation Nick had left when he opted out of her life.

What, she wondered, did Dr Harley De Winton want of her? It bothered her. She found his gentle concern as hard to assimilate as the anger he had let loose that day on the lake. He was behaving as if they were on the same level, which was not ethical if they were to work in the same hospital.

The train ponderously clung somehow to the tracks, throwing her against the partition, making her even more aware of him on the other side of it. Was he asleep or, like her, wondering how they were going to get through the working day which lay ahead of them both?

It was no use. She would never sleep now. Outside was still only blackness through which the train ploughed on, still swaying sickeningly. Why had no one warned her? But Oliver had . . . She smiled then, in spite of herself. No one had forced her to come. But neither would she have missed this journey for the world.

Glancing at her watch, she saw that it was already four-thirty and they started serving breakfast at six, so she read for a time until it became light enough outside to see something of the passing scenery.

The day began with a grey misty breaking of cloud and the landscape was shrouded in a cold, bleak loneliness of wilderness and endless forests. A moose stood alone in a river, the only sign of life, gazing forlornly at the passing train. Crossing over the river on the bridge was a noisy experience—the Fraser rushing below, rather awesome.

She longed for some hot coffee, deciding to get ready so that she could go along to the early breakfast as soon as it was time.

When she was dressed, in a cream polo-necked sweater over beige slacks, she quietly opened her door.

No one else seemed to be stirring as she went along the corridors to reach the dining-room. Here, a sleepy redcap emerged from his cubby-hole, looking at her impatiently.

'Good morning,' Philippa greeted him. 'Can I have some coffee—or early breakfast?'

'Breakfast is served at six,' he informed her testily.

'It is almost six.'

'Then you can't have put your watch back, ma'am. There's an hour's difference in time between Alberta and British Columbia. It's barely five . . .'

'Oh—no. What about coffee?'

'I'll bring some to your couchette when it gets going,' he told her. 'Number six, isn't it?'

'Yes . . .' she said wearily as she retraced her steps, past the still sleeping passengers in the coaches who hadn't, like her, the privacy of a couchette.

She felt annoyed that Harley De Winton hadn't warned her of the time zoning. He was probably catching up on his sleep in there, she thought angrily as she reached his door.

But it opened suddenly, almost as if he knew she was there, which he couldn't have, and he stepped into the corridor wearing only a brown towelling short robe on his way to a room opposite marked 'Bathroom'.

Before she could speak, the train lurched, throwing them against each other. He held on to her longer than he need have, his eyes full of devilry, until they half closed as if he had made some kind of discovery in that brief encounter. Philippa, unable to prevent a tell-tale flush creeping over her face, opened her own door. The close proximity of his lean body through the robe against her was very revealing and she hoped, only to herself.

Her blush had amused him and he didn't intend to lose anything of the situation, so he questioned her as to where she had been that early. Philippa looked back over her shoulder, taking refuge in finding something to come back at him with.

'To the dining-car, for breakfast, and I think you might have told me about the hour's difference in time, Dr De Winton.'

'Oh—no . . . Did you really?' He grinned delightedly. 'I guess they weren't very polite to you. That's hilarious.'

But she had closed her door with a loud slam, for once in her life acting selfishly towards other passengers not yet up. So—he thought it hilarious, which fact did nothing to improve her temper after the sleepless night.

Half an hour later she heard a tap on her door and, thinking it was the coffee she had ordered, opened it to find, instead of the redcap, a freshly groomed, somewhat chastened surgeon, regarding her solemnly, a coffee tray in his hands.

CHAPTER FOUR

'CAN I come in?'

She stood back so that he was able to squeeze into the very limited space between the double seat and the washbasin.

'Hadn't you better sit down?'

There was a short pause while he regarded her solemnly. 'Only if you will. Breakfast should be starting soon and I'll take you along with me this time,' he said firmly.

She saw a mischievous glint appear in the dark eyes and felt that absurd tremor again. In spite of herself, she murmured, 'You're laughing at me again.'

'Of course not. I came to apologise actually. Sit down.'

Crossing one beige-clad leg over the other, he turned to regard her more seriously. 'I hadn't realised that you aren't yet used to some things over here and I'm feeling responsible. But you coped remarkably well in the hospital with what must have been a different routine and techniques and a completely strange environment, so it didn't occur to me that . . .'

'Hospitals,' she said briefly, 'are not very different. Only people. Perhaps because at home we have the NHS patients are not so demanding. People expect more over here, I think.'

'And usually get it.'

A thought entered her mind and she voiced it. 'Did you arrange to be on this train, Dr De Winton?' she asked reflectively. 'I mean . . .'

'I know what you mean, Nurse Croft.' Again his eyes regarded her lazily. 'I've decided to call you Philippa. Only until we arrive, of course—okay?'

'If you prefer it,' she said simply. 'But you haven't answered my question.'

'I do prefer it. And I did make a special effort to be on this train when it became apparent that I might make it after all. The emergency call from Dale Bonek came just after I had called you at the hospital. He sent his two-seater plane for me which meant that I could choose to return by train. It is new territory for you and the journey can get very boring; besides, I was grateful for your quick decision to come up here and take over my father. I want him to live a bit longer if it's at all possible. I think you may be instrumental in that, if anyone can.'

A peremptory knock on the door announcing that breakfast was being served took them out into the corridor and along to the dining-room. They sat opposite each other, although she was still loath to meet his eyes. She found it difficult to drink her orange juice in the jolting sway of the train.

'Is it always like this?'

'I don't usually do it this way,' he told her, 'but I guess so. It's a single track.'

The scene outside was changing now but still sparsely populated; just a landscape of sprawling hamlets interspersed with dark green trees, very tall trees of spruce and larchpole. There was snow too, piled along the sides of the track and she remembered Oliver's words.

'I wasn't really expecting to see snow,' she said. 'My brother-in-law warned me but it seemed so late in the year for it.'

'It shouldn't last too long. The temperature is a bit low though.' He was looking at her intently.

She lowered her eyes to her plate, spreading marmalade with a slightly unsteady hand, knowing instinctively what he was going to ask her.

'What prompted you to come to Canada? Something must have precipitated your leaving a hospital where you were obviously quite happy. Not wanderlust, surely?'

'Do I have to give a reason?'

'No. If you prefer not to. But I should have thought you had reached promotion standards. Yet you were still a staff nurse.'

'I had,' she admitted. 'I would have been made Sister in Charge at the end of the summer.'

'Then—why?' His voice was gentle, bringing a rush of nostalgia to her throat.

'My reasons were personal,' she admitted. 'I made a sudden decision when they were needing SRNs over here and it all happened rather quickly after that. I'm not sorry—don't think that.'

'And Edmonton was your choice because of your sister and her family being there?'

She nodded. 'Yes.'

'You can always go back there, you know.'

She smiled at him across the table. 'I've a job to do here first,' she said firmly. 'How much further is it?'

As he glanced at his watch, she found her eyes fascinated by the dark hairs on his wrist.

'We should arrive around seven-fifteen. Now—details of where you are going to stay, Philippa.'

'But—I thought I would report to the hospital and hopefully have a room at a hostel. Should I go straight there? Or is it rather a different procedure as I'm specialling only Mr De Winton?'

'Yes—it is.' He had been watching her with a patiently amused expression but now she paused and he took over.

'We have an apartment which is used by any one of the family needing to stay in Prince George, or visiting business associates of my father who also like to use it sometimes. My secretary has left the keys for you with the janitor and checked, I hope, that you have everything you need.'

She opened her mouth to say something, but he went on.

'This is on my father's express order so you need have no reticence about going there and, as I said, everything else should have been taken care of. The hospital is a few minutes away so it is quite convenient.'

Her eyes opened to their bluest dimensions. 'Good heavens—and I was expecting to have to find somewhere or move in with the other staff. But I'm not sure I can take advantage of Mr De Winton's offer. After all . . .'

'I think you must accede to what he wants for the present, don't you? It's probably been good for his morale to take care of this for you. And you'll obviously want somewhere to go when you're off duty. I'll take you there initially and then you are free to do as you please.'

'I see.' And up to a point she did, but she wasn't too sure that she wanted her independence to be wafted away like this. She could, of course, make other arrangements when she knew her way around perhaps. And now there was no more time because the train had slowed down even more and buildings appeared on either side—scattered wooden shacks and taller blocks of apartments.

'This is the downtown area,' Dr De Winton said briefly as he opened the door for her to go through. 'Your luggage will be put in the waiting-room so we just have to collect our hand luggage and get off. Oh . . .' he smiled again in a more friendly way this time, 'welcome to Prince George, Nurse Croft.'

An icy blast of freezing air caught her hair as she stepped down from the height of the train, at least three feet above platform level, and Harley De Winton, having shrugged himself into a suede jacket, strode along by her side, shepherding her into a huge waiting-room where a very mixed crowd of passengers were also awaiting the arrival of their luggage on the conveyor.

She was delighted to see her two brown cases appear for the first time since leaving Edmonton and to hear him directing a porter to carry them out to a yellow cab at the kerb. Inside they were thrown together as the driver drove around the block and out on to the highway; Philippa looking with interest at the varied shops and offices and yards along the way, and noticing to what extent wood had been used in the structure of this town.

'It's much larger than I thought,' she murmured, for the second time righting herself after their shoulders collided. He disregarded the flush that rosied her cheeks as he said nonchalantly that Prince George was the largest town on Highway 16.

She felt that should mean something.

He went on to explain. 'Last night we came through the Yellowhead Pass, towards Yellowhead on the borders of Alberta and British Columbia. Right?'

She nodded. 'Yes.'

'You remember the bridge over the Fraser River? That was when we actually entered Prince George, which was established as a fur trading town way back in the seventeen-hundreds by explorer Simon Fraser. He founded Fort George. It goes on from there.'

'Interesting,' she admitted, 'because Canadian history is comparatively new, isn't it?'

'But fast-moving, that's for sure. Ah—here we are.'

She thought the apartment block looked rather affluent but said nothing as she followed him out of the car.

'Wait for me,' Harley commanded. 'I want to go on to Mackenzie Court.'

The yellow cab driver carried her cases into the foyer and the janitor handed the surgeon an envelope containing the keys.

'All yours,' the surgeon said briefly. 'He will carry your luggage up to the apartment. I have to be at the hospital by eight-thirty and I guess you do too. So . . .' he glanced at his watch, 'I'll see you later. Oh—it's number seven, Philippa.'

He was gone, with long strides, towards the waiting cab, leaving her standing alone in the carpeted foyer. Then she followed the janitor up one flight of stairs to the first floor.

Number seven loomed in front of her. He turned for her keys, unlocked the door and deposited her bags on the green hall carpet.

'Thank you.'

'That's okay, Ma'am.' But she thought his glance was a little curious.

No wonder, when she was the new resident in this luxurious apartment, paid for by Clyde De Winton, and everyone knew that he was not amiss to installing a lady here from time to time. Although this one looked a bit on the young side. Besides, he'd heard the old guy had a heart attack down in Alberta. Still—it was no business of his and all in the family, because the surgeon seemed to know her pretty well.

Wandering through the apartment, Philippa was enveloped in warmth, the double-glazed windows shutting out the chill wind. Her watch hands pointed to seven forty-five. Dared she risk a bath in the green marbled bathroom where soft, warm towels were ready for her?

There was no time for luxuriating and quickly she unpacked the immediate things she would need. In the small kitchen she discovered coffee and a carton of milk and quite a small store of food. Someone had been very thoughtful indeed. Tomorrow, she would probably go shopping on her own account.

The coffee revived her. Soon afterwards she went down into the street, her hair pinned neatly into a fold at the back of her head and, crossing the street, made her way to the hospital entrance, anxious now to see her patient and start her new duties. She needed purpose in her life, discipline and routine, and she felt a little like the engineless boat that day on the lake, until she knew just what was expected of her in yet another strange hospital.

The freezingly cold morning was even more noticeable after the warmth of the apartment and she walked briskly towards the main entrance. To the left of the door Emergency was situated, its huge letters in red glass still shining bright from the night. An ambulance passed while another was just leaving. Two cars swept into the parking-lot, their occupants looking important enough to be registrars or even surgeons. The lighted windows showed patients already seated in the various clinics and it looked, as it was, a very busy place to be.

Crossing the recently defrosted tarmac she saw a long brown car coming from behind the car-park, turning into one of the reserved spaces for the consultants. Dr De Winton, changed now, climbed out and went into the hospital by a different unmarked white door. He hadn't seen her and probably wasn't even looking, she told herself, just a little disappointed. She would have liked to go in with him. Even remembering his lofty status, he might at least have pointed her in the right direction to

where she must report. But his patients were waiting.
She could see his name above the door. They sat in
plastic chairs, bandaged, some with walking aids, in
wheelchairs; others just patiently waiting while the
nurses checked them in. His day had truly begun, as hers
was about to do. She wished she knew her way around
because it took her quite a few minutes to find the office
she was looking for and make herself known to the
secretary in charge.

When she was admitted into the office, she knew at
once that this was just a formality.

'Do you have your own uniform?' she was asked.

'Yes, Ma'am.' She saw the other glance over her black
cloak with its red lining.

'I understand you have already been nursing Mr De
Winton in Edmonton.'

'Yes.'

'So you will know that he isn't the easiest of patients.'

Philippa smiled. 'Yes, I know that.'

'A bit unorthodox bringing you all this way too—but
he is getting through nurses like a bear with a currant
bun . . .' She stood up. 'We're glad to have you, Nurse
Croft. Dr Gurnett is in charge of the case. You will find
Mr De Winton in room twenty-five. You will report to
Dr Gurnett personally but any problems—I'm here in
my office. If you need assistance, just ask for it. I believe
Dr De Winton will be keeping in touch as well. You do
have some accommodation, I take it?'

'Yes, Ma'am. I'm very comfortable, thank you.'

'Good. Then go along and see your patient, Nurse.
I'm quite sure he is waiting somewhat impatiently for
you.' She spoke into a communicating intercom on her
desk. 'Julie, come and take Nurse Croft along to room
twenty-five, will you?'

Then, looking across at Philippa, 'You're out from the

UK, I hear. That's interesting. We must get together some time and compare notes. If you're at a loose end any time, just let me know. Ah—here's Julie. Mr De Winton's room.'

'Thank you very much,' Philippa said gratefully, surprised at being on equal terms with the Nursing Matron, with whom one had lived in awe back at St Andrew's. As she went with the girl along various passages and corridors, she wondered at her new position even more. Brought here by a consultant surgeon; housed in a luxury flat and now being given almost VIP treatment! Mr De Winton must indeed be rather a special person around here she decided as she entered his room quietly, in case he was sleeping. But he had been sitting up watching the door expectantly for quite some time.

'Hullo,' she said brightly.

'So—you're here at last,' he said in the husky voice she knew. It still lacked strength and she thought he hadn't progressed at all. She must look at his notes as soon as possible.

'How are you feeling now?' she asked, after a quick smile at the nurse putting his toilet things away.

'Not fast enough . . .' His breathing was laboured. 'I'm—glad you—could make it. You are going to stay . . . ?'

'Yes. I'm here to stay.'

He looked drained, his face thinner, his moustache neatly clipped though, and his thick hair brushed into a silver wave on his forehead. He was still a handsome man.

'I'll be back . . .' she said softly, 'just want a word with your nurse, Mr De Winton,' going across to her table.

'I'm Nurse Roberts.'

'Nurse Croft.'

'Yes, I know. I wondered what you'd look like. He's

been asking for you all the time. You are really something as far as he's concerned.'

'Difficult that. Makes one feel inadequate, doesn't it?' Philippa said softly. 'I've had the same experience myself. But you'll be still sharing the duties, won't you?'

'I'll be stepping in for you and doing the late evenings. I don't mind. It helps me to be at home all day. I've got a couple of kids.'

'Oh, I see. Perhaps I could see his notes—before you go.'

'They're in the file. Dr Gurnett will be in around ten o'clock. Everything else is fairly straightforward. Clean pyjamas, etcetera in those two drawers. Oh—he prefers to use his own towels; and he is a bit fussy about being washed.'

'I know. There is a male nurse available, isn't there?'

'If you catch him early.'

'Okay. Thanks.'

'Have you two finished whispering about me?' Clyde De Winton asked testily from his bed. 'Come back over here and tell me what's going on.'

Philippa went over to him while Nurse Roberts disappeared through the door.

'I'm just catching myself up to date,' she told him quietly. 'How do I know what you've been up to since you left Edmonton?'

'Not very much—I can tell you. They're trying to keep me wrapped in cottonwool. Damned ridiculous thing to do. Harley's as bad as the rest of 'em. Did you come up with him?'

'Yes. And—thank you for lending me your apartment. It's very comfortable—I feel quite spoiled. And it's so close to the hospital.'

'That,' he said with an attempt to look wicked, 'was the general idea.'

'There's hope for you yet, Mr De Winton—I can see that,' she said smiling. 'Have you had breakfast?'

'Just juice and toast.'

'That isn't enough.'

'What do you suggest then? I guess I'd like a mug of coffee you could stand the spoon up in.'

Her fingers slipped across the radial artery on his wrist and it was quiet in the room except for his breathing as she lifted the watch on her breast to count the seconds. It was natural that it should be uneven, especially today, but it was still much too fast. She would like to talk to his doctor but meanwhile there was still the file to be read thoroughly, which the other nurse had left on the table for her.

'Is there anything you want immediately?' she asked, straightening his sheet and making his head more comfortable on the pillows.

'Everything. But nothing that I can have . . .'

'Oh—you are feeling sorry for yourself. I'll get you up after Dr Gurnett has been in, then we can see what can be done to cheer you up a bit.'

'I've got to get out of here . . .' he said confidentially. 'They're making an invalid of me. See what you can do. Talk to Harley—I've got to know what the score is. Lying here, listening to my own heartbeats is lethal.'

It was, she agreed, although she only gave him a comforting squeeze of his hand before going over to look at his file. As a patient he presented a real challenge. She had been a little shocked at the way he looked now; and she had to do something about that. He was dying, as much from fears about himself as his deteriorating heart condition.

The report sheets in his file only confirmed this. The damage was very extensive, and she would need to be on the alert for further complications because his coronary had been caused by atheroma of his arteries in the first instance. But why, she wondered, hadn't Harley suspected that his father was hypertensive? Maybe he had but Clyde refused to take medical advice and his son could hardly drag him to the hospital or even his doctor.

He was a very sick man and, as such, she was going to have a difficult time keeping him from any excitement, chill or too much heat—and especially the thrill of risk-taking which made life worth living for him.

Dr Gurnett confirmed her findings. 'We'll just have to do what we can, Nurse. He can stabilise enough to go home but that's where the trouble begins again.'

'On the other hand,' she mused, 'why shouldn't he be where he is happiest, whatever the resultant issue.'

In the afternoon, Clyde had a visitor.

'Brett,' he shouted. 'I hoped you'd make it today. Come in, boy. What do you think of my nurse? Didn't I tell you she was an English rose?'

Philippa went quickly to his bed-chair. 'Mr De Winton—you're getting much too excited,' she said firmly. 'Take your tablets, please.'

'She's also—a bit of a tyrant . . .'

Philippa looked up apologetically into the toughened face of the broad-shouldered Canadian who still stood turning his stetson hat in his hands, not entirely at ease.

'I'm sorry. But he does have to be kept fairly quiet, I'm afraid,' she reminded him.

'Oh, sure. I understand that.' They looked at each other briefly, each with their own thoughts about the other. She liked his weather-toughened face, though his eyes were almost unreadable. She pulled up a chair for him near to the patient's lounger and bent to tuck the blanket more firmly around his legs.

'My second son . . .' he told her with some pride. 'Brett De Winton.'

She noticed that he hadn't said adopted son—as Harley had.

'Hullo, again,' she said laughingly.

'Hi . . .'

'So what goes, Brett? Did you get those heifers branded and out on the range like we said?'

'Drove 'em out yesterday, though I still think it's a bit early. There's a lot of snow around in the foothills. Still—you're the boss. They were sure glad to be out there on the loose. We'll keep an eye on 'em for a day or two though, I guess.'

'Ahh . . .' he said impatiently. 'They're hardy enough. We can talk business in front of this nurse of mine, Brett. There was something else I wanted you to look into. Have you brought in my mail?'

'No.'

'Why the hell not?'

'I guess there was nothing I couldn't attend to, and you're still convalescing.'

Philippa, noticing the restless twitching of her patient's hands and that his colour was rising, stepped in then.

'I really think you should go now,' she said quietly but significantly. Brett's face in profile closely resembled his father's, the same heavier build too. As he got to his feet she knew that he was right out of his habitat and it showed.

'You don't have to go yet.' Clyde De Winton hated to be thwarted in anything. 'You've only just got here.'

'Get some rest,' Brett told him, his voice almost as husky as his father's. 'I'll see you again in a couple of days. Just get fit and come home.'

'I want that more than anything.' The tired eyes clouded over and as he watched his son go to the door she knew he wouldn't improve very much until he was back there again. Frustration was nagging him and his BP fluctuating because of it. More than anything, he needed to be untroubled, ideally calm and patient. He was neither.

While he slept during the early evening Harley came in quietly. Because he wore a white coat, having only recently finished his reports, Philippa felt a widening gap between his world and hers. Yet it was simpler for the doctor-nurse relationship to be adhered to than it was earlier that same morning when she had surprised herself, or her body had, to her consternation, by being physically attracted to this man. His masculinity was still very obvious but now there were more pressing matters. The clinical environment and the seriousness of the patient's condition merited serious and controlled thinking.

His worried frown was back as he met her eyes over the file as he handed it back.

'Has he been out today, Nurse?'

'For about two hours. It was long enough, I think.'

'Mmm . . .'

The voice from the bed told her that Clyde was no longer dozing. 'Hey, you two . . .' he said sleepily. 'In a huddle again? If it concerns me—I want to know.'

'It doesn't,' Harley said firmly. 'I'm trying to persuade Nurse Croft to have supper with me.'

Clyde chuckled—while Philippa opened her mouth in surprise at the audacity of his quick thinking. He wasn't serious, of course. But she was mistaken, because his expression conveyed that he was.

'Will you?' he asked, raising his eyebrows slightly.

Having only had a sandwich for her lunch because she hadn't wanted to leave her patient for too long, she was hungry now. His invitation appealed strongly and she

nodded her head, blushing a little when she said, 'Yes—
I'd love to. Thank you very much.'

'Good. I'll pick you up around seven. Okay? I'm not
changing.'

'Fine. I'll have to I think, but nothing dramatic.'

While he sat with her patient she went to check on the
drug supply, making sure that everything was there for
the night staff to take over. The hospital was used to
patients from all over the territory which was widely
scattered and in some places extremely barren and
lonely. Emergencies and after-care were as in England
but what was different was that there were no practices
or doctors' surgeries as at home. One phoned the hospital and simply came in. She had discovered too that OR
was another name for operating theatre, and EKG
meant electrocardiograph.

As she hurried back to the block of apartments after
being relieved from duty, she had only half an hour
before he came to collect her. 'Don't change,' he had
said, but she couldn't possibly go out without at least a
change of clothes. She smelled of antiseptics, or hadn't
he noticed? And she must also phone Emma. She would
do that first.

Her sister sounded relieved that she had arrived safely
but was a bit sceptical when she heard about the apartment.

'Watch it, honey,' she advised. 'If you plan on staying
up there, I'd get one of my own and be independent.
Well, at least I have your phone number.'

Philippa hadn't thought it necessary to tell her that she
was going out to dinner with Harley De Winton. She
shook out a lacy-knitted suit in a lovely shade of blue
which matched her eyes, and after ten minutes in the
bathroom, brushing her hair until it gleamed like silk,
she fastened the frilled neck and pulled on grey suede

boots which fitted her legs perfectly. A quick spray of *Je Reviens* perfume, a real luxury, which she had bought at the airport on her way over, did a great deal to inspire confidence in her new image. She wasn't used to dining with top surgeons and this particular one evoked an uncertainty in either her own or his reactions in different situations.

He was lord of his domain here at this hospital, she had discovered in only one day. And if it wasn't that his father had confidence in her, hating the ministrations of other nurses around him, Harley De Winton would never have noticed her. His eyes missed nothing. She would hate to be on the receiving end of his temper if she were caught side-slipping. One of the other nurses had given her that information as they returned from their break.

'You know who he is, don't you?' She had indicated the card on her patient's room door. 'Dr De Winton's father . . .'

'Yes. I do know,' she affirmed. 'I nursed him in Edmonton.'

'Then I don't have to warn you to be on your toes. He can slay you with just one look over the top of his mask in theatre. You should watch one of his ops some time. It's a revelation. Theatre Sister adores him. But it's hell if you make any mistakes or break his concentration. He looks as if he's about to throw the instrument at you. But—oh boy—he's a charmer when he wants to be.'

As if she didn't know that, Philippa mused, feeling refreshed and looking forward now to going out for a meal. Especially with the kind of man who would simply take over. Why—she wondered—had he suggested it? Surely there were other girls who would jump at the chance of sharing his evening.

A charmer—the other nurse had called him. A little

tingle of pleasure rippled along her spine. Warning signals tapped at her instinctive reticence. She must not even begin to think of him in that context but keep a tight control over her emotions, as she had done since they had taken such a devastating bashing from Nick's callous breaking away. Never, she told herself firmly, would she let herself get in that deep again, but neither could she be flirtatious or indulge in casual sex. Oh, Nick, I hate you for what you've done to me, she thought miserably. How could I have let you?

Her eyes were bright from unshed tears as she stood there remembering.

The door bell, pealing softly through the apartment, broke her reverie; an unhealthy one which she regretted having slipped into. Tossing her hair back, she went to the door.

But Harley De Winton had no intention of letting her thoughts be anywhere but on him. Stepping into the hallway, openly appraising her before holding her coat while she slid her arms into it, he appreciated the difference it made to feel the softness of her beneath his hands and be very aware, not for the first time, that she possessed all the attributes he admired most in a woman.

'I like your perfume. It's just right for you,' he said with a disarming smile as he opened the door and followed her down the stairs to the long brown car at the kerb.

She smiled but made no answer. It was a nice way to start the evening nevertheless.

CHAPTER FIVE

HARLEY was intrigued with this girl who had so dramatically come into his life that day on the lake. He had an entirely wrong impression of her in the beginning but now he had to admit, if only to himself, that she had grown on him, almost without his being aware of it. He hadn't any obligatory reason for planning to be on that night train from Jasper, yet he had used every artifice to make it, once he knew it was a possibility. His patient's two-seater plane was at his disposal to fly back to Prince George but he had chosen to drive like crazy into Jasper, arriving in the nick of time to find her, surrounded by all the other passengers; the girl with moonlight on her hair. The wave of male protectiveness which pushed him forward towards her was quite a new approach for him, used as he was to having women friends at the end of a telephone wire and he even admitted to some cynicism about their willingness to meet him more than half-way.

But this girl was different. She showed no sign of wanting to fall into his arms. He felt instead an urge to be dominant and break through the shell she was protecting herself with. Yet, even the way she shyly avoided his eyes, since Jasper, could be construed as an indication she wasn't exactly immune, surely? It might be interesting to find out.

Their table was in an alcove where the soft glow of the wall lights caught her hair as she studied the menu. He was preoccupied with her femininity—the soft blue of her wool suit clung to her figure excitingly. The female

76

form held no secrets for him, but neither had he ever allowed himself to become blasé about it. He was much too good a doctor for that.

Suddenly she looked up, surprising the expression on his face and, for a moment, their eyes met. Then the moment was dispelled by him asking easily,

'Have you chosen? I'm having T-bone steak with all the accompaniments, I think. And I thought salmon mousse to begin. Is that okay for you?'

'Oh, yes. And I'm dreadfully hungry so could I have the steak too?' She felt like a small girl at a picnic. He thought so too because he smiled indulgently.

'Of course. And we need some wine to revive us. I guess we have both had quite a traumatic twenty-four hours. Oh—here's Carlos . . .'

The wine ordered and a few words to the waiter, then they had time for more appraisal of each other. She saw his eyes travelling over her face and neck and down to her clasped hands on the table, pink nails to match her lipstick.

'You're staring at me,' she said gently.

'I know. I'm curious about you, Philippa. Tell me about yourself.'

'You make me feel like a new patient starting out on a history questionnaire,' she chuckled, her eyes dancing now.

'Except that this is much more exciting.' She saw the mischief lurking in his brown eyes. 'And I won't have to write it all down; it's just for my ears.'

His eyes held hers deliberately. Was he getting the same waves across the table? she mused as the waiter arrived with their mousse and the words hung suspended.

'So?' he probed when they were alone. 'If you really don't want to talk about your reasons for coming to

Canada—okay—just say so. Is it something you want to forget?'

She drew in her breath sharply. Of course, she was here to forget Nick, but to discuss him with Harley De Winton was out of the question. She refused to be drawn. It was no business of his. Surely he hadn't brought her here to appease his curiosity.

Carlos chose that moment to appear with a wine bottle in his hand, which Harley approved, and she watched as her glass was filled. She sipped it appreciatively.

'It's nice and robust . . .' she observed.

'You know about wine?' Harley asked.

Nodding, she explained. 'My parents have an hotel on the cliffs in Cornwall. I was brought up in that background. Yes—I know a good wine when I taste it. So do you . . .'

'Good.' They were on the same footing now. 'So—tell me some more about you.'

'What—' she asked, looking down at her plate and pushing her fork into her mousse '—do you want to know?'

'What you are running away from, Philippa,' he said softly.

He had touched a raw nerve and her reaction was resentment towards him.

'Do you mind if we don't pursue this any further?'

He apologised. 'I'm sorry. It was unforgivable of me. But you are rather an unusual person, you know. You arouse my curiosity.' He didn't add that she also aroused the primeval instincts peculiar to every man, no matter how well camouflaged by a sophisticated veneer. It always came down to basic instincts. But there was something pure and guileless about this girl which evoked his protective instincts too. Her face came into his inner vision more often than he would admit and it wasn't mere curiosity that had prompted his questioning. He was selfish about his relationships with women usually, his passionate nature taking him where he chose, but he also steered clear of a too-enveloping relationship—except perhaps Rachel—but even with her—he promised nothing.

He had been ruminating for almost five minutes, without realising it, while he ate his mousse, and Philippa wondered if it was because she was reluctant to talk about her decision to come to Canada. But the arrival of their huge platters of steak and mushrooms and crisp side-salads, made the rest of the meal very enjoyable. The wine helped, of course, so that her cheeks were flushed when they at last left to go out into the cold night and she was in a lighter frame of mind.

While they drove through the lighted streets to the apartment block, he talked about his father. After all, he was the reason why she was here. It sobered them both and when he asked if she would consider going to the ranch with him when he was fit to do so she didn't even hesitate. There were too many reasons why she must see this special case through. By now, if it was important to Harley, it was important to her. She was caught up in something which seemed to be taking her along on a buoyant wave—predestined; no ordinary nursing care, which she would have given to any one of the patients who passed through her hands on the wards. She felt personally involved in Mr Clyde De Winton because she respected his approach to what he knew could be his curtains. He had reached out to her so that only she had been allowed to see the tears he was too weak to hold back those first days. It was she who gently wiped them away so that no one else saw or suspected that strong men sometimes cry.

'We're here . . .' his son was saying. 'Were you asleep?'

'No – of course not.' But she hadn't even known the car had stopped.

He leaned across to open her door, then got out himself. 'I'll come up with you.'

She felt too exhausted now to protest, even if she'd wanted to. Her one thought was that she could soon crawl into bed and get the sleep she craved.

Taking her key, he opened the door and followed her inside.

'Okay – I've no intention of staying,' he muttered, his mouth twisting into a half-smile. 'I'm exhausted too. Have you got everything you need?'

'Yes . . .' She came back to where he stood looking down at her laconically. 'I'm sorry – do you want coffee or anything?'

'Not anything,' he assured her gently, 'except perhaps . . . this . . .'

Slipping one hand at the base of her neck, he drew her face forward close to his, finding her lips softly tremulous beneath his questing mouth, and only letting her go just when she ached for him to continue so that she closed her eyes for a moment, needing to recover, when his fingers slid away.

'Get some rest . . .' he advised throatily, even abruptly, which she hadn't quite expected; then he walked quickly back through the still open door.

Philippa watched his long legs take the stairs two at a time, before she closed it, to stand with both hands pressed against her flushed cheeks disbelievingly. Yet it had happened. His kiss, still excitingly warm on her lips.

I didn't even say thank you, she thought ruefully. And after all the care he had taken with their meal.

It was still only ten o'clock but she was desperate for

some sleep now so she undressed quickly and went into the bathroom, surprised when she saw herself in the mirror. Her eyes were luminous, her face rosily pink and as she brushed her hair the thought hit her. The impossible had happened. She was falling in love again, differently, but in love, with Harley De Winton. She hadn't wanted to resist him tonight. She admitted to herself quite honestly that she was already waiting for him to kiss her again. And more than once – more than just a goodnight kiss. And did he feel like that too? Or was it just the time and place and perhaps because he thought she had expected it? Heaven forbid . . .

Five minutes after slipping into bed and pulling the gorgeously soft duvet over her shoulders, she was asleep and didn't waken until the alarm rang at six next morning.

Stretching deliciously after a deeply restful sleep, she padded into the kitchen and filled the kettle and only then remembered Harley's kiss. But not only that, the way all her senses had responded to it. Did he remember too?

She arrived at the hospital in good time, changing into her white uniform and cap and pulling off her suede boots, bending to tie the laces on the comfortable white ward shoes. She wondered how Mr De Winton was feeling this morning, remembering that she hadn't thanked him personally for the watch on her breast. Just a letter from the Edmonton Hospital – which he probably hadn't been well enough to bother with.

But she was wrong. It was in his wallet in the drawer of his locker. And he had reached this morning of his own accord to retrieve it and read it through again. Philippa had become for him more than just a nurse. She was someone he could trust to tell him the truth, help allay his most elemental fears, be comforting in a warm, human way. He needed her hands, caring hands; her voice, even when she spoke softly, was reassuring and while he hadn't even thought of having to convalesce at home, if he made it, that was, he had made up his mind to ask Harley to invite her there some time. He would like to see her there at the ranch.

Now, as she breezed into his room with her smile for him already reaching her eyes, he held out his hand for her to grasp.

'What a long night it's been,' he said breathlessly. She heard fluid in his chest and he coughed drily.

'How are you feeling today?' she asked, careful not to let him see her concern. Alert for complications, she was looking for symptoms such as dyspnoea, as she asked carefully, 'Any pain?'

'Just a little – here . . .'

Substernal pain with dyspnoea could mean a pulmonary embolism. Oh God – she hoped not. Not now that he had survived the worst and was on his way towards some kind of recovery.

Refusing to let him even suspect that all was not well, she joked and told him that she had had dinner with Harley last night.

'I'm glad to – hear it. You'll be cutting Rachel out if he's that interested in you; that's – for – sure.'

His hand flew to his chest as he struggled for more breath. She didn't hesitate, lifting the phone to ask for his doctor to come immediately. Also, Sister in Charge whom she hadn't so far seen because she was not returning from her weekend leave until this morning.

They both arrived at the same time and Dr Gurnett administered nitrites immediately and gradually the attack subsided. But they all knew that it was probably the first of many and the patient would have to know his limitations. He could not expect to return to the normal life he had lived until now. But who – Philippa wondered, as she cleared up afterwards – was going to tell him.

All this was going to prolong his hospitalisation which would react on him frustration-wise. Ideally, he should be kept placid, his whole outlook channelled into acceptance of his changed lifestyle. Which was the hardest thing in the world for Clyde De Winton to do. She wished Harley would come but he was operating all day and they couldn't hope to see him until later.

She knew that Clyde De Winton was awake and lying there watching her while she arranged some white spring flowers and freesias which had come from his Edmonton friends but she thought him disinclined to talk so pretended that she thought him still asleep until, as she put them where he could see them, he said huskily,

'Come over here.'

She did so.

'What,' he asked miserably, 'happens now?' He looked worriedly into her face. 'Sit down – talk to me. That was a bad one, wasn't it? I thought – I was – finished that time. I can't live with the uncertainty of not knowing – when these damned attacks are going to happen. What do I do about it? Help me . . .'

He reached for her hand. Unhesitatingly she slipped hers into his huge one, softer now than the work-roughened hands he had before his coronary.

'No exertion . . .' she began. 'Try to let things go over your head for a while – just be patient and gradually you will find yourself returning to near normal. Give it time, Mr De Winton. You've been very ill.'

'Will I ever be anything like the man I was, Nurse? No – I can see you know I'll never ride out with the boys and rope a steer or round up the cattle for the winter. In which case – I may as well be dead.'

'I don't know what you will be able to do when you've recovered,' she said honestly, her voice full of compassion. 'But if you want to do something hard enough, who knows? The important thing is to get you walking again. This attack was a warning that you still need lots of bed-rest. So we'll take it slowly and when Dr Gurnett thinks you can move around more and you can go to the bathroom on your own, I expect you will go home.'

'Will you come with me?' It was the man and not the patient asking her this. She heard the despair in his voice. 'Will you?' His fingers tightened. 'Don't run out on me; I'm going to need to talk to someone I can trust not to spill the beans. There's no way they're going to think they've an invalid up at the ranch house for a boss. You can take over the medication and check me out, can't you? Harley can keep an eye on me when he comes out to Rouen's Creek. I'll pay you any salary you want – just don't run out on me. Not until it's time.'

What did he mean by that, she wondered, as she gently disengaged her hand and stood up, looking down at him with sympathy and understanding.

'You don't have to offer more money, Mr De Winton,' she reassured him. 'The important thing is for you to be seeing a maintained improvement. That will be the best therapy you can possibly have. And as for coming with you—I did promise your son last evening that I would, if at all possible, see you through this unsettling period and if it means coming out to your home then I'll try to do that.' He seemed content with that.

Harley came straight over after his last patient had gone from theatre to the recovery room. He had removed his mask but still wore the green cap and long gown. Philippa, who had been waiting to see him, felt an instant glow deep inside her body. She wanted to talk to him first but he strode over to the bed to say teasingly,

'So—what have you been up to, Father? Giving every-one another scare?'

He hadn't looked at her once and Philippa, who had been filling in her report, now got up and came over to the bed.

Clyde looked anxiously up at her. 'Did you tell him what happened?' he said huskily.

'I think Dr De Winton will already have seen Dr Gurnett.'

He didn't comment but he was assessing his father as he would have any other patient.

It occurred to Philippa that he was avoiding looking at her. It was definitely a doctor-nurse situation: all the protocol being strictly adhered to.

'I'd like to see the file, Nurse—all the same,' he said, glancing across at her as he spoke, his voice crisp and positive.

She brought it to him and there was silence in the room while he ran his eyes down the page.

'Thanks,' he said shortly, handing it back. Then, with a quick gesture, he pressed his father's shoulder, 'I have to go—got a meeting at five. I may possibly come in again afterwards. Take it easily—get some sleep if you can—okay? And stop fretting . . .'

'Okay,' came the disgruntled voice from the bed.

'Thanks,' Harley said shortly, looking in Philippa's direction, but not at her, before his green-gowned figure disappeared through the door.

Disappointment swept through her. What had she expected? A continuation of last night? He had behaved impeccably just now. Did she think he would have reminded her of their last moments together? Perhaps he preferred to forget that he had kissed her like that. Or was he so exhausted after his terribly long list in theatre that the two things refused to come together? Just a smile—anything would have done, she thought, perplexed by his apparent disregard. It was as if he had decided that from now on they were to be on a professional footing only and last night was just his way of showing appreciation of her coming to Prince George.

And now, she would simply carry on with her job. It was, after all, Mr De Winton who was paying her salary, not his son. And he was looking a bit down in the mouth too.

But it was Harley of whom he was thinking just then, voicing his thoughts as he so often did to her.

'I guess he's had a bad day too,' he said thoughtfully, 'or did something go wrong with you two last night? You know you haven't spoken of it all day? And he was definitely off you.'

She bent her head over the finished report which Charge Sister had asked to see before she left.

'There hasn't been too much time,' she reminded him, while she closed the file and got up slowly before coming over to the bed with it in her hands. 'As soon as I got here you decided to instigate a flap in the ward—remember? Had us running around in circles for a time. And I haven't thanked you for providing me with such grand accommodation either. I didn't expect you to do anything like that. I could have gone into the hostel.'

'I only suggested it. Harley did the rest. It's not in use—why shouldn't you use it? Did something go wrong with you two last night?' he ended on a curious note, his breathing laboured again.

'Why should it have? He gave me a lovely meal and left me at the apartment around ten. Your son is a very clever surgeon, Mr De Winton, and he has probably seen twice as many patients today than he should have and had as many operative ones as could be fitted in. He's got a backlog, I believe.'

She shouldn't have said that. She realised it immediately. Clyde would blame himself for that.

'I'm glad you're feeling better tonight,' she went on, her voice softened more than she knew to his receptive ears. 'Now we have to snap you out of the doldrums and see that it doesn't happen again.' He saw her mouth curve into a smile.

'And how do you intend to do that?' he murmured quizzically, captivated, as others had been, by the way a smile lit up her eyes too.

'By avoiding people or problems which make your blood pressure go sky-high,' she told him truthfully. 'By seeing that you have adequate rest, eat only small meals, take your medication at the right times, do gentle exercise and keep calm. Also—I shall remind you that every day you behave is one day nearer to your going home.'

'Gee—that sounds good. But the rest is boring. Will I survive it?'

'You will. I'm going to see that you do. It's what you pay me for—isn't it?'

'You're not mercenary. Money isn't that important to you, is it?'

She shook her head, relieved that she had drawn some response from him. He was now answering her smile, rather as one smiles at a child to reassure him, in the same way. The next moment he had relaxed enough to doze into a restful sleep. Going to the door, Philippa closed it softly behind her and, at the end of the corridor, asked one of the nurses who was not busy to keep an eye on her patient while she went to see Sister in her office.

'Come on in—you have left someone with him, Nurse Croft, haven't you?'

'Yes, Sister. One of the nurses outside.'

'Good. I'm sorry we haven't got together before this morning's episode but, as you know, it was my long weekend.'

Philippa waited while she reached out for the file. 'You can leave this with me. I'll return it when I go. What is your own assessment of Mr De Winton?'

Philippa went into technical terms to describe his condition and the complications she was on the alert for. She was also put in the picture a little more by Sister's direct knowledge of Dr Gurnett's prognosis, which only confirmed her own. It was something accepted among the nursing staff, especially the seniors, that nurses often knew as much as the doctor in some cases. Which made it simpler to carry out instructions and look for certain warnings which a visiting doctor couldn't be expected to know about.

All this had been incorporated into her training which was why she could behave naturally with doctors now and not, as she sometimes recalled ruefully, trembling each time one spoke to her, blushing bright pink if a consultant even said 'good morning' and fearful of dropping an instrument or mucking up a sterile pack on her first day on theatre duty.

'Okay Nurse, you'll soon be off now then. I'll come and have a look at Mr De Winton before I leave. Has his son been in?'

This was asked casually but Philippa sensed that there was more behind the question. Was Sister another of his adoring female staff?

'Yes, he has,' she answered noncommittally.

'What did he say?'

'Only that his father should stop fretting and get as much rest as possible.'

'Not very helpful when a man is as frightened as Mr Clyde.'

'You've noticed too.'

'Oh, yes. Before you came he even showed withdrawal symptoms—nobody got through—not even Dr De Winton.'

'I saw that in his notes.'

'So—you've come a long way with him in a couple of days, I suppose. I think he'll make it now.'

'I hope so . . .' Philippa spoke from her heart. She felt very close to Clyde De Winton; almost as if his reliance on her was becoming a bond between them. And if she was able to help him get back to the ranch again, guide him to cope with and accept the proposed different lifestyle which was the most he could expect—then the challenge she had set herself would have been won.

It was warm outside as she walked back to the apartment. The snow was beginning to turn to slush and causing a few accidents judging by the activity over at the Emergency entrance. Even as she reached the street, another ambulance skidded on the wet surface as it turned into the hospital precinct. Harley's car, brown and sleek, was still in the parking-lot. His registrars would have to cope with the new admissions if they were orthopaedic but often, with multiple injuries, the residents were involved and the top men consulted yet again, even coming back to the hospital after a gruelling day.

While she was free to spend the rest of her evening any way she liked. Which for Philippa meant an early night after some disappointing television and perusal of some of the magazines she discovered stacked neatly in the lounge. Why, she wondered, would they be women's magazines? She couldn't really imagine the rancher on his occasional trips to Prince George, settling down with *Woman's Journal*.

But she found them interesting and after phoning Emma and hearing Danny's voice insisting that he said 'Hi . . .' to her and asking when she would be back, she felt less out of habitat and much more relaxed in this rather bewildering town which hadn't quite the same friendliness of Edmonton somehow.

All evening Philippa had steered her thoughts clear of Harley De Winton's attitude towards her in his father's room. For whose benefit had he switched off her? His own, his father's or to remind her of the protocol which must be adhered to?

Yet why had he bothered to take her to dinner last night? It hadn't been necessary. And it wouldn't have mattered to anyone if he had given her just one look which said he hadn't forgotten the train journey, his gentleness last evening and his kiss. Had she responded too much, too quickly? She couldn't even remember. Only the impact of his lips on hers. The way he had looked afterwards before he left so abruptly.

She didn't want an affair with the man any more than he, she thought angrily, as she stared now at the reflection of the passing headlights on the curtains. So—tomorrow, when he came to see his father, she would show him that she too knew the rules and would be very careful about implementing them.

And next morning, when he caught up with her in the foyer, following her into the same elevator, she waited for him to speak first, determined not to be persuaded away from her set course, refusing to look up at him, contenting herself instead with staring down at his shoes. Until he broke the silence, except for the elevator mechanism.

'Good morning,' he said, 'or isn't it?'

'Good morning, Dr De Winton,' she said briefly, meeting his eyes a little rebelliously.

Eyebrows raised he commented, 'It isn't. Nothing wrong, is there?'

'Nothing—thank you,' she answered as the elevator stopped and she got out without a backward glance.

That would show him that she had no designs on him and didn't intend to take advantage of anything which may have happened previously. Her job was to take special care of his father. This she intended to do but for only as long as absolutely necessary.

Clyde was looking rather fragile today. He had lost some weight and needed reassurance even about that. It was out of context, this anxiety, because from all sources she knew that he was normally such a positive, go-getting person. Stronger than most in character.

'Harley tells me that Brett will be over again today,' he greeted her when she returned from her coffee break.

So he had been in while she was away which was strange because he had a long list of clinic patients, judging by those still sitting waiting for him.

'That's nice,' she said brightly. 'Perhaps you will be able to talk a little more this afternoon—and not get het up—because, if you do . . .' she threatened, 'he will have to go again.'

'You're a dragon—underneath that girlish image,' he groaned.

She saw his eyes assessing her with the hint of male devilry which had probably been an essential part of his make-up.

'You are feeling better,' she told him as she prepared to take his BP, finding it up on yesterday but inclined to fluctuate, which was better than shooting up and staying there.

When all her chores had been completed and Dr Gurnett had been in with his intern and there was nothing more to do for her patient for a while, she came to sit beside his bed after putting his pillows in his favourite armchair position.

He looked less grey now, his hair brushed into place, but almost silver. He wore his pyjama coat open at the neck, brown and well-tailored.

'You look very smart today. You're sure it is only Brett who is coming?'

'Oh, sure. And he doesn't leave the ranch unless he has to. Except for me, I guess.'

'Oh? Is there anyone else there? Who looks after the house and everything?'

'Aileen does that. She's a damned good cook and an excellent housekeeper. My wife taught her all she knows.'

His eyes clouded suddenly.

'I'm sorry,' Philippa said quietly, 'I shouldn't have asked.'

'Of course you should. You're coming back with me, aren't you? You heard what Dr Gurnett said. That's the only condition—they'll let me go. As if they could keep me here if I decided to discharge myself.'

'You wouldn't do that?'

'No. Of course not. Besides—Harley's here too.'

'Does your housekeeper live at the house?'

'Oh—sure. She's got her own rooms off the end of the veranda—she and Maura—her small daughter.'

'No husband?'

'No.' He declined to enlarge on that.

The door opened to admit Charge Sister. 'Am I intruding?' Her eyes flashed a significant glare at Philippa before she came up to the bed, giving the patient the benefit of her sparkly brown eyes.

'How are you today, Mr De Winton?'

'I feel—fine.'

'I'm glad to hear it. You're going to be allowed out

again tomorrow, Dr Gurnett tells me.'

'Yes—another step towards going back to the ranch, Sister.'

'I hope so, and I also hear that you're taking Nurse Croft with you.'

'That's for sure,' he said throatily. 'Which makes everything okay, doesn't it?'

'I guess it does,' she answered without hesitation.

While both she and Philippa knew that his condition was anything but 'okay' as he put it. In fact it was going to be a day-to-day situation for all concerned with Clyde De Winton in the coming months.

CHAPTER SIX

SPRING and summer seemed to arrive together. One morning a bright sun shone from a clear blue sky as Philippa left the apartment and she noticed that the tight buds on the aspen trees, grouped around the drive-in, had opened to the warmth, their sweet scent reaching her as she walked towards the street. Tourists had come to Prince George too, stopping over on their way west to the Rockies.

She had discovered her way around town now and was getting invited to social evenings or dances with other nurses from the hospital. There had been no more meetings with Harley De Winton outside the hospital and indeed he seemed to adhere strictly to the normal doctor-nurse relationship now whenever he visited his father and she was there, calling her Nurse Croft in the kind of voice he used to any other nurse with whom he had to communicate.

Which proved she had been right. He had wanted to get back to a more ethical footing. The train episode was over.

But this morning, he came across to the table where she was writing down the time of Clyde's last medication. Closing the file, she stood up and surprised the frowning look from under his almost black eyebrows. Then he picked up the file himself instead of asking for it as he usually did.

'Has Dr Gurnett spoken to you yet?' he asked quietly.
'About what?'
'He thinks my father may be allowed to go home at the

weekend. This is off the record, of course.'

She met his eyes; the brown irises held darker flecks, more apparent today, and the moment she discovered that, little exciting tremors made themselves felt and she had to do something about it. She took a step backwards. But she had to look at him again when he said softly,

'Are you still prepared to go out to the ranch with him?'

'Yes. Of course. Did you think I would go back on my word, Dr De Winton?'

'No . . .' His eyes were searching hers now and a kind of indignation was taking over from the more intimate impact of a moment ago, as she faced him reproachfully.

He still hesitated before replying. 'No . . .' he repeated slowly, 'but I thought you might have had second thoughts and weren't very sure what to do about it. I'm glad you haven't . . .'

They both glanced over to the chair near the window where his father lay back quietly with his eyes closed.

'He doesn't know yet?' she murmured.

'No. Dr Gurnett wants an assessment done today before making his final decision. I just thought I should warn you if you did want to change your plans.'

'Thank you, but nothing has changed. I'm glad he may be discharged soon—I don't think he could hold out much longer. This will give him some hope—he's a bit low-spirited today.'

'I'm aware of that . . .' he said crisply.

They were mistaken in thinking that Clyde was dozing. He called testily, 'What are you two whispering about over there—and what are you aware of, Harley?'

They walked over to him together. Clyde, wearing a green silk dressing-gown over cream pyjamas and looking groomed, though grey-tinged and older, gazed up at them rebelliously.

'Well?'

'Nurse Croft tells me that you walked a few steps this morning. Not going to take off on your own, are you?'

'You knew that already. What else were you discussing, or isn't it any of my business?'

Philippa broke in then. 'Dr De Winton was just making sure that I still want to come with you when you go home.'

'We know the answer, don't we? You do . . .'

'Yes. Of course,' she said clearly. 'I'm looking forward to it.'

'You and me both,' he muttered. 'I can't wait to get my pants on and my saddle boots. And talking of pants, Harley. Can you get me some new ones? My girth has changed somewhat—that's for sure. Three inches less at least. Better take the measurements.'

'Typical . . .' Harley smiled as he went towards the door. 'Right now, I've got to see patients, Father. Your nurse will measure you for some new ones,' he threw Philippa a conspiratorial glance. 'You might need them sooner than you think and Clyde De Winton has never yet been caught with his pants down—to my knowledge. So get on with it.'

His father's chuckle was like a shot in the arm as he made his way towards the elevator. Thank God the immediate emergency was over. There was not very much anyone could do about the future, other than what they were already doing. Right now, he needed to switch off completely and prepare himself to listen to his patients' problems and/or progress. In fact, the rest of the day would be exhausting enough with the decisions he must make: to operate or not; to recall his experienced years of surgery; to know just what to do in any given circumstance or set of symptoms. Ten minutes later he was sitting at his desk, studying a patient's X-ray picture, everything else eliminated from his mind.

Back in the room upstairs Philippa was quietly going through her patient's belongings, making sure that everything would be back from the laundry by the weekend, just in case they should get an all clear. She was feeling much happier now that Harley had broken the ice again. It was still important to him that she should go with his father to the ranch, but how conformist of Clyde to expect him to go shopping for pants—ignoring his commitments as an orthopaedic surgeon. She had seen it only too often. Older patients were much more demanding than younger ones and their own weaknesses used as a cover-up to sheer moral blackmail.

Not that Harley would let that happen. But already his father had claimed his vacation period, or most of it, and he would expect Harley to drive out to the ranch as often as possible. But she would see him too. Because there was no doubt how much she wanted to see him now. Just to be with him for a short while was enough to brighten her whole day. And as long as he had no idea of this, what did it matter? She had made her decision never to fall in love with a doctor ever again; but that was exactly what she was doing. Only this time, he need never know and there would be no humiliating ending. Just her own ruthless cutting him out of her life, when the time came to return to Edmonton and eventually England. By which time she would have made a few decisions about the furtherance of her own career. But now, she was going to take one day at a time and just see what evolved.

Before Philippa left the hospital that evening, Charge Sister sent for her and told her that Clyde De Winton was to be allowed to go home.

'Dr Gurnett has made the decision reluctantly,' she said, 'but he does seem to be stabilised now and it will be your job to see that he continues to make progress. Though to what level is anybody's guess. He will have a word with you himself but your patient is going to have to live a restricted life, very different from his previous lifestyle, and come to terms with his limitations. It isn't going to make your task any easier, Nurse Croft. You'll have to be constantly on the alert for complications. There's always the possibility of cardiac failure, as you're aware.'

'I understand that, Sister. It's a continuation of what I have already been doing. The only difference, I won't have a resuscitation team in the background. Just me and the telephone.'

'You're sure you know what you're taking on?' Sister asked sceptically.

'I think so.'

'And you don't mind being so far out there in the sticks?'

'I don't have any idea how far it is actually,' Philippa commented. 'But it has to be within reach of civilisation.'

'Oh, sure, it's within reach . . .' She drew in her breath. 'Well—you've taken this patient on and I know you'll see it through. Rather you than me. But, good luck, and you will certainly enjoy the surrounding country out there. Maybe we'll see you back here again some time.'

'I shouldn't think so,' Philippa said. 'I'm due back in Edmonton after this case is finished, but thanks—all the same.'

Coming out into a slightly misty evening after a day of rising temperatures, she breathed deeply of the first air of summer. Harley's car was not in its usual space, she noticed, so he must have left early tonight. Did he know of the decision to release his father, she wondered. But of course he did and probably had been consulted. He just hadn't bothered to tell her though. Should she have expected him to? And how soon would they be leaving for the ranch? Days—hours?

Deciding to check out her uniform which she intended to wear while at Rouen's Creek, for more than one reason, she first washed and then slipped into a sprigged flowered housecoat. She laid her clothes on the bed, then reached for her suitcase, but decided instead to have something to eat before continuing her packing.

Supper consisted of a feather-light omelette and some fruit. Then she made coffee and carried it into the bedroom with her before making another start on her packing.

Switching on the radio, she found herself humming along with the orchestra's rendering of 'Canadian Sunset', only too appropriate this evening as she was drawn to the window by the spectacular flame of colour streaking the sky away to the west. Tonight's colour was phenomenal and she was conscious of feeling very small fry as she gazed at the purple and orange slashes behind the hills.

When the doorbell pealed her heart seemed to stop. It could only be one person. She had forgotten her bare feet as she padded across the deep pile of the carpet. There was nothing she could do about the fact that she was wearing her cotton housecoat, she decided philosophically, nor that her heart was beating wildly as she turned the brass lock-sprung door handle and opened it.

'Hullo there. Were you going out?'

She shook her head. 'I was, but I thought I should get some packing done. Do come in, if you don't mind this . . .'

She indicated her housecoat as she stood back for him, blushing a little helplessly.

'No. I like what I see . . .' he said, grinning delightedly, as he looked down at her bare feet and pink-tipped toes peeping from under the lace-frilled edging.

'I'll go and change,' she faltered.

'That won't be necessary. I'm on my way over to a colleague but as I had to come this way, I thought we might talk about getting Dad back to the ranch. You do know that he is being discharged?' he added, as an afterthought, as she followed him into the lounge.

'Yes. Charge Sister told me tonight. But not when. Or hasn't that been decided yet? By the way—would you like some coffee? It won't take a moment.'

He shook his head as he sank into the comfort of the velvet chair and crossed one leg over the other. He still kept on his suede jacket, though, beneath which a cream silky polo-necked sweater only heightened his dark eyes as he looked up at her speculatively. 'I'm not sure we aren't expecting too much of you, Philippa. It's just that he has become rather dependent upon having you around. And this, for him, is absolutely out of character. Oh—sit down. I can't talk to you while you're still standing and I'm expected on the outskirts of town in half an hour.'

She curled her feet under her as she sat down obediently on the settee opposite him, aware of his eyes running over her amusedly now.

'Oh . . .' she burst out exasperatedly. 'This is ridiculous—trying to have any sort of conversation with me dressed like this.'

'Undressed, you mean, don't you?' he amended lazily. 'But I don't object—so why should you? I told you —I like what I see. You look quite delectable as a matter of fact.'

'Oh . . .'

Rosy colour suffused her face, even her neck, emphasised by the crisp white lace around the edge. Her hair was softly curling to her shoulders but now she tossed it back and resolutely made herself meet his equivocal look, calling up all her resources and asking quietly, but firmly,

'When are we to go?'

'I guess I'm being remiss, I thought you knew. On Friday—I shall be free after my clinic—say around two-thirty.'

'You're coming with us?' Her eyes lit up.

'Of course. I shall have until Sunday night, when I must drive back here, to see that he settles in. It will make the move less traumatic, don't you think?'

'Oh, yes. I'm so glad that you're coming too. I—wish I had known . . .'

'Why?' he was curious after that unexpected and spontaneous reaction.

'He will settle better, knowing you're around for one thing.' She didn't enlarge on that, even though he waited.

'And you, Philippa? Will you settle in better if I'm around?'

She knew he was sounding her out so parried his question with one of her own, sliding away from the teasing note in his voice.

'Charge Sister warned me that we shall be out in the sticks—whatever that means. How far and how long is the journey going to take? I need to know.'

'It will probably seem like the back of beyond to you. I forget that you are new to this territory. The ranch is about thirty kilometres from the highway; just this side of Quesnel. I expect it will take us all of two hours to reach it, though I can do it in less when I'm on my own. I should warn you, if no one else has, that you need to stock up on anything you might want personally. There's no corner shop—just a trading post out on the highway. Quesnel is the nearest town. But you drive, don't you? In the winter it's difficult, sometimes impossible to get off the ranch when the snow becomes ice-packed, but right now it should be looking green and lush and I'm looking forward to being there again for a couple of days. It's home, I guess. I was born there.'

'But you left it to go to university?'

'I knew what I wanted to do with my life before I was twelve. Nothing's changed.'

She smiled at him, a little tremulously, moved by his depth of feeling which he made no attempt to hide from her.

'I still love to go back,' he said, unwinding his legs and getting to his feet. 'Oh—just one more thing—Dr Gurnett will give you a list of drugs and put you in the picture, of course. There will be an ambulance laid on—I've arranged that, and any other preparations are left in your hands. Any queries?'

His mood had changed back to the more normal one she understood.

He flexed his wide shoulders and she noticed now there were tired lines around his eyes and chin, removed only when he smiled a little wearily down at her before she too got to her feet.

'No queries,' she said, shaking her head.

'Right. Goodnight then, Philippa. I'll see myself out.'

He was gone. She stood looking at the closed door for a full minute, her lips pursed thoughtfully, before she could gather herself together and go back to her packing. It had been rather nice to see him sitting there in the armchair, she mused, and it was even nicer to know that he would be coming with them on Friday. He had reverted to calling her Philippa again too. What an enigma of a man—she never knew how he would be—or what to expect of him from one hour to the next. Yet tonight—she had felt that he was relaxed with her, trusting her to help him cope with a loved, but not entirely easy, parent. And he would be there—within reach—for the whole of one weekend. It was an exciting prospect, to say the least.

She went breezily into Clyde's room next morning, expecting him to greet her on the same level, but he was testy and morose because he hadn't yet been told the result of his assessment. Philippa tried to raise his spirits but it was difficult. When Dr Gurnett came at around ten o'clock she heaved a sigh of relief.

Clyde was already out of bed, having shuffled the three steps to his chair, holding on grimly to Philippa's arm. He barely acknowledged the consultant's 'Hullo, there,' until he stood looking down at him speculatively before saying gently, 'I've got news for you.'

Philippa saw the apprehension growing in Clyde's eyes and wished his doctor would get on with it.

Putting the notes on the bed, he heard Clyde's voice rasp out, without even turning his head, 'Well—get on with it—tell me the worst—it shouldn't take long.'

'Okay. You're going home, Mr De Winton. Day after tomorrow. On one condition—you adhere strictly to instructions—and do what Nurse Croft says—all the way along.'

Clyde closed his eyes, relief spreading through him, and Philippa, standing close by, saw his struggle with emotion at the news he had dared not hope for. She guessed he had steeled himself for more disappointment and his voice was husky when he murmured, 'Thanks,' before looking up at her. 'Did you hear that, Nurse? We're going home.'

Before she could reply, Dr Gurnett broke in. 'I must make a few things clear, Mr De Winton. You're going to have to accept a changed lifestyle. No exertion—a lot of rest—and a slow convalescence: for another three months at least. After that—we'll see. Nurse Croft will keep me informed of your progress. Harley too will take a look at you from time to time. If you want me—I'll even come out to look at you myself. What I don't want is to see you back here again. It's up to you.'

Clyde frowned. 'No horse-back riding . . . ?'

'Certainly not.'

'Nor—steer chasing?'

'No. But you knew that already.'

'I guess so. So what can I expect?'

Dr Gurnett went into details about the heart muscle which hadn't recovered full power yet. That medicines were imperative and there would be dietary restrictions.

'You can still enjoy life,' he went on. 'Don't be too pessimistic of the future—and we'll see how you progress.'

'It hardly seems worth it,' Clyde said moodily after the consultant had gone. 'What does he know about what constitutes enjoyment in my life? Does Harley know yet? He hasn't been in . . .'

'Yes, he does. And he intends to travel with you.'

'That's just great,' Clyde was obviously pleased about that, looking up at her with an odd expression which she couldn't quite understand—a kind of speculative one. She had seen it before, on the train from Jasper, when his son had looked at her in exactly the same way.

A nurse peeped round the door. 'Can Dr Gurnett have a word?' she said softly. 'He's in Sister's room.'

He was waiting, fitting her into his busy schedule as if he had all the time in the world.

'Ah—Nurse—I'll let you have the final analysis before the end of the day on Mr De Winton but I thought we should have a few words together. You're in this on your own, I'm afraid, except that I'm on the end of the telephone if you need advice. In any case, I want a weekly report for the next month. You know the sort of thing. And I think he may need some physiotherapy. Can you manage the exercises and get his leg muscles active again?'

'Yes, sir.'

'Right. His condition is a serious one—and will not, I think, improve very much. With this kind of prognosis you'll have constantly to check him out and be on the alert. In three months he should be as good as he's ever going to be, or totally unable to accept that he's an invalid. I'm sure you can cope—are you sure you want to?'

'Yes, Dr Gurnett. I understand the situation and Mr Clyde trusts me. If anyone can help him to adjust, I think I can.'

'Remember then—call me if you need advice, or Dr Barnes. You're not entirely on your own, Nurse Croft.'

'Thank you, sir.'

He's nice, she thought, as she went back along the quiet corridor to room twenty-five. Most nurses would agree that the higher the status in the medical profession, usually it meant the nicer the man. And as she looked down into the well of the hospital, she saw Dr De Winton speaking to one of the nurses and as he did so, one of the patients sitting on a plastic chair struggled to get to his feet, dropping his crutch as he tried, and it was Harley who jumped forward and gave him a steadying hand while the nurse picked it up.

Suddenly a wave of such intense feeling surged through her, she felt the impact physically, putting her hand on the rail to steady herself. She almost groaned aloud at the ignominy of it. She had run away from one doctor only to let herself become submerged by another and this one, impossibly out of reach. Oh—he liked to flirt a little—and snatch a kiss and run—but she had no illusions about the kind of woman he would choose for his wife, if he ever got around to it.

She would be a doctor too and share his interests both in the hospital and away from it. She would be clever and they would have dark-haired children who resembled their father. That is—if he ever got around to giving up his freedom.

So—what was she griping about? For forty-eight hours she would see him off duty—relaxed—as he had been that day on the lake. Heavens—how angry he had been with her then, she thought, as she went rather guiltily back to her patient, conscious of having stayed away a bit longer than she should have.

Harley came during the afternoon, sitting with his arm along his father's chair while they discussed arrangements for the journey.

When he had gone his father observed, 'Harley's in a good mood. He called you Philippa—did you notice? Not the first time, I guess . . .'

'I—didn't notice. And I expect he's happy because you are going home and he is having a brief holiday.'

Clyde chuckled. 'Maybe . . .' he said mysteriously. 'That's not the only reason if I know anything about it.'

It was a lovely evening and the traffic was heavy as she walked along the side-walk on her way to the stores. The sun was warm on her face although the mist was already hovering over the hills and she wondered idly if there were hills or even mountains at Rouen's Creek. By the name, she would think there was a river or a lake of some kind. It would be exciting to see it for the first time.

A greyhound coach stopped at the traffic lights on its way to the bus station, having come all the way from Vancouver that day. It was a good way to travel, she thought idly. Maybe she'd do that before she went back to England.

Behind the coach a long brown car, sleek and impressive, which she immediately recognised, also slid to a halt. Harley was driving a passenger, one of the doctors on the women's surgical floor. Her dark short hair cut in a kind of wedge style, fell provocatively over one eye as she turned to say something at which they both laughed, before he bent his head to look up at the overhead lights preparatory to shooting forward again.

Well—perhaps that was his type of woman—elfin-faced, petite—and very clever. They were enjoying being together, that was evident. So—why did it have to matter quite so much? And why had the sun chosen that moment to disappear in a shroud of mist? The background music in the shops was too loud, the lights too glaringly bright and she had forgotten her shopping list so it took twice as long to go back and forth to find what she could remember from it.

Trudging back to the apartment she knew she had no right to resent the way Harley and his colleague were laughing together, enjoying the moment. Sour grapes—she told herself angrily. And what Harley does in his spare time does not concern you.

To break her train of thought she glanced up at the tall, modern buildings on either side of the highway. How it had progressed over the last few years. The down-town area especially, the buildings rising in layers and becoming quite thickly populated it seemed. Yet outside—it was still a near wilderness.

She was certainly in unfamiliar territory and in a day or two even more strange and new experiences were coming her way. She supposed that Brett lived at the ranch house—and Aileen, as she already knew, and Harley—when he was home. But there had to be others around. The cow-hands, drovers and their wives—if they were married. It might even prove to be quite a community. The thought raised her spirits considerably.

Back at the apartment she washed her hair, blow drying it until it shone with golden highlights then, with her supper tray on her lap, she watched scientists discussing the changing weather pattern from the Arctic ice floe on TV. Would there be another ice age, she wondered, following their remarks seriously. It was too interesting to switch off but did nothing for her restless mood. She should have asked a few of the other nurses over for the evening. Perhaps tomorrow night, as it was her last, but she decided that it would be too much to clear up after they left. She must leave the apartment exactly as she had found it. Who knew what new occupant would use it, or when? Not Clyde, that was almost certain. But what of his friends—the ones who liked women's fashion magazines—she thought wickedly.

Emma—she must let her know where she would be after tomorrow.

'Are you surprised?' she said, laughing after a pause followed her announcement that she was about to disappear into the back of beyond.

'Nothing you do surprises me any more,' Emma said philosophically. 'But, keep in touch. Give me your phone number as soon as you arrive. Where is it?'

'Rouen's Creek—that's all I know. The De Winton

ranch, I suppose. Oh—it's caribou country—Mr De Winton did tell me that.'

'Rouen's Creek,' her sister repeated aloud and Philippa distinctly heard Oliver's voice in the background,

'My God—that's right out in the sticks. She won't wear that for long.'

'I heard that,' she said ruefully. 'Does he think I'll chicken out then?'

'I guess he does,' Emma agreed. 'Have you written or phoned home yet?'

'No,' Philippa confessed. 'I'll do it tonight.'

'Well—call us when you arrive there. Might not be too bad with the summer coming on—and Phil—don't get carried away by those burly cowboys, will you? Some of those ranch hands are real he-men, I've heard.'

'No chance—if her doctor is anywhere around,' Oliver put in, laughing over the wire. 'Just keep both feet on the ground, honey, and we're here—if you need us.'

'Thanks, Oliver,' she said fervently, feeling even more apprehensive about the unknown territory she was about to discover for herself.

On Friday afternoon Clyde was taken down to the car-ambulance at the side doors of the hospital, with Philippa close behind carrying a rug for him and her medical bag.

'I can't believe it's happening at last,' he said, a little emotionally, turning to wave to the other staff who had come to see him leave, as Philippa climbed in beside him.

Then he leaned back on his pillows, his face grey with the effort of leaving his room and the excitement of his send off.

'Rest now,' she ordered. 'You can watch the sign-posts. I expect you'll recognise them all.'

'Every one,' he said simply. 'Is Harley behind us?'

'No—he is just about to overtake us,' she confirmed as his car set the pace and they followed behind.

She had been too concerned with her patient to notice Harley's movements before this but now she saw his dark head and straight shoulders ahead. He wore a brown silk shirt, open at the neck and he drove steadily out into the main stream of traffic and soon a pattern of scenery took shape which, in a way, prepared Philippa for the kind of loneliness to be found in this part of the world.

'Red Rock . . .' Clyde said with a happy grin. 'We're sure heading the right way now.'

But—was she?

CHAPTER SEVEN

THE highway stretched endlessly between forests of spruce trees, tall and dark against the sky. It all seemed so desolate to Philippa, just as it had on the other side of Prince George when she viewed it from the train. It was hard to assimilate the vastness of the area, coming as she had from her home on the coast in the west of England. A gasoline station by the side of the road had a solitary wooden house behind it. She wondered what they did for neighbours and how they survived when frozen up in the winters, or if someone was ill, for instance. Further on, a derelict homestead, little more than a log cabin, was still standing, the interwoven logs at each corner holding up part of the roof—grim reminders of occupants who had at last fled in despair. Imagine having children born there, with no one to help. What courage and tenacity they must have had. What terrible privations too.

Clyde noticed her expression as her imagination went to work. She could somehow identify with them.

'You'll see quite a few of those around. All the way along the Cariboo trail, in fact . . .' he remarked.

'How did they survive?'

'Kept on fighting, till it wore 'em down. Maybe they'd have a horse and a cow and grow their own food and scratch a living, but there was usually no future in it and they started to move into settlements and that way built up a life for themselves. Quite a few still farm the places their grandfathers started in the early eighteen-hundreds. They even had their own cemeteries too, and built schools, mainly just wooden huts but a kind of community centre, and made a trading post here and there. You'll see tiny churches too as you go further south.'

'There were the fur traders too, weren't there?'

'Oh, sure. Anything was done to make a living: fishing, trapping, either for barter or cash. Cattle too. It was tough going, but some of 'em made it.'

He lay back on his pillow. She hated to see the blueness around his mouth and the pallor of his skin as she watched him turn his face away from her.

'How do you feel?' she asked gently.

'Tired, I guess. God—I hope this exhaustion will pass.'

'Of course it will. It's quite a big day for you, one way and another. Rest for a little while.'

He was already dozing into one of his catnaps and she unobtrusively slipped her fingers over his wrist.

He must not have too much excitement today, she decided, her eyes following the car in front and wondering if Harley would stop soon for a break.

A few miles further on he did so, turning on to an unpaved stretch of road, little more than a track wide enough to take a car or truck, and drew in beneath the trees. As the ambulance came to a halt beside him he stepped out on to the grass, flexing his arms and taking deep breaths of pure pine-forest air.

When he came over to them her heart jumped a beat again. She let down the window and got out.

'How is he?' he asked briefly.

'Still sleeping but doing very well actually. Much better than I imagined. He's a bit tired, naturally, but then it seems to be quite a long way for him on his first day. Is it much further?'

'Around thirty kilometres. We are almost on his

territory now. It probably appears longer to you, does it?'

'I expect I'm concerned for your father. That's why it does. Oh—he's just waking . . .' She turned to go back to the car and as Harley followed she said quietly, 'He tends to be a little confused still when he wakes up.'

'What's wrong? Why are we stopped?' Clyde wanted to know.

'Nothing is wrong, Dad. We're on the lake road now, almost home. I just stopped for a break. We can push on if you're okay.'

The driver, who had also stretched his muscles, got back in, declining Philippa's offer of juice or coffee which she had thoughtfully brought with her, as did Harley and his father, preferring to wait until they arrived at the ranch.

Clyde was peering into the trees. 'Can you see old Joss around, Harley?' he said firmly.

'No—I don't see him.'

'Who is Joss?' Philippa asked curiously.

'Joss is an old guy who's been around here a lot longer than I have,' Clyde told her. 'He lives in that cabin in the trees. You can just see the top of it.'

'Alone?'

'He's something of a character,' Harley explained, 'and spends his time either panning for gold-dust in the streams or the creek and trapping.'

Philippa frowned. 'Is that still done? I thought . . .'

'It's the way he lives,' Harley said.

'And when it comes to trapping beaver he's the best there is . . .' his father put in.

'Oh . . .' Philippa looked a little distressed at that, which Harley noticed.

'There is a beaver lodge on the river and we don't know how many families live and multiply under the banks but they block it so that it overflows, especially in the spring run-off. They do an awful lot of damage to the trees too, gnawing right through them—so sometimes a beaver cull is necessary.'

Clyde was restless. 'Can't we get on now?' he asked testily.

'Okay. You're the boss,' Harley agreed.

'That's right. And don't let anyone forget it.'

Philippa and his son exchanged tolerant glances and each got back into their respective seats and soon they were driving along a road, little more than a track, with trees on one side and a sheer drop on the other. Now and then she caught the glint of sunbeams on the water running over the stones, winding past a tiny cabin and, up in the trees, the remains of a tiny church.

'There used to be an Indian village along by the river,' Clyde explained, seeing her interest quicken as she leaned forward.

'This really was Indian country then?'

He nodded. 'They are mostly living on reservations now though. There's one not far from us. Some of the children go to the same school as Aileen's child.'

'You mean, their parents live on reservations while the children attend school with the others?'

'Of course. Some of my best friends were Indian. One especially—he taught me most I ever knew about raising cattle. The rest I learned the hard way, by making mistakes.'

'You're talking too much,' she said gently, as she saw his fingers gripping the rug over his knees excitedly, while his eyes darted from one side of the track to the other.

'I know—but it's the time I've dreamed of, isn't it?' he murmured disarmingly.

Each twist in the lane took Harley out of sight. Each

time Philippa waited for him to reappear. It was wonderful that he would be at the ranch too all the weekend. She had never been near him for a long period. Besides, there was something rather more intimate about living in the same house.

His car had stopped. She saw one of the ranch hands, wearing a checked shirt and with a stetson on his neck, leave his horse tethered to a tree and run forward to lift the white pole stretched across the road which barred their way.

As the brown car swung forward he raised his hand to Harley but his eyes were mainly on the ambulance. His wide grin was welcome enough for his boss but he saw him waving his hat in the air when they passed and knew that he was home at last. On his own ground.

A long drive led up to the house with ranch fences on either side and cattle grazing in the meadows. The river narrowed and wound through the valley and, in the distance, were the mountains, still snow-tipped and even from there, reflecting dazzlingly in the sun.

'It's beautiful . . .' she breathed, 'and so peaceful—I didn't realise . . .'

Turning to look at him, she saw there were unashamed tears in his eyes. 'I never thought . . .' he started to say, but couldn't go on.

'That you would see it again?' she finished gently. 'Well—here you are—home at last. And you're going to really enjoy that. I can see the house . . .'

He was still gazing unbelievingly, shaking his head from side to side. It was all too much, and as they swept up on to the gravel frontage it was as if the ranch homestead was waiting for him, its windows shining in the sun; the huge logs which had gone into building it, burnished and mellow, seasoned by storms and snows. The roof came right down to three feet from the veranda which seemed to run all around it. She knew that was to let the snow run off, which was why the windows were well back too. A huge door stood open and Brett was first through it, coming down to help with the chair she had brought for Clyde.

Harley was already opening the door. 'Well—what do you think of it?' he asked close to her ear as he leaned forward.

'I love it . . .' she said simply.

'Here come the staff, Dad—you've got a welcome home party by the look of it.'

Ranch hands came from the stables, the sheds, the feed stores and she saw a generating plant in one of the outhouses as she climbed out.

'I'd no idea it was such a community,' she told Harley. 'There's so much going on. I hope it isn't going to be too much for him.'

'We'll get him into the house as soon as possible, I think,' his son was observing him as he was lifted into his chair.

'Those steps—he shouldn't . . .'

'They won't let him.' He hurried over to speak to Brett who immediately had one of the hands grasp the other end of the chair while he took the top and Clyde, still protesting, was pushed into the house.

A woman came from the kitchen as they reached it whom Philippa guessed must be Aileen. She was right and Harley introduced them.

'Aileen—I want you to meet someone very special. This is Nurse Croft.'

'Hullo,' Philippa said, smiling in her friendly fashion, not knowing what it did for her as her eyes twinkled with deeper blue flecks in the irises and her teeth positively gleamed.

Aileen simply nodded shyly.

'Boss is home, Aileen,' Harley said brightly as the noise from the sitting-room grew more rumbustious. 'I think it's time to break that up, don't you, Nurse?'

Philippa shook her head helplessly. 'Can you do it?' she asked, 'because I don't think they would hear me.'

Aileen had gone into the kitchen to rescue the coffee but now rejoined them saying simply, 'It's good to have him back.'

Brett came out into the hall then, Philippa saw that he had removed his stetson and it had left a pink rim across his forehead. 'He's demanding drinks all round,' he told them sceptically. 'I guess that's out.'

'Definitely,' Harley affirmed.

'Right.' He went back into the room where Clyde was firing questions at his men, positively revelling in the situation.

'He'll be quite shattered,' Philippa said, looking a little anxiously at Harley but attempting then to hide a little smile when Brett said authoritatively,

'Okay—back to work. Drinks all round this evening. Guess we should celebrate Boss's return, but right now he needs some rest.'

And ignoring Clyde's shout of protest, he ushered them all outside and their boots clattered down the wooden steps.

Philippa followed Harley into the large, comfortably furnished room, where a log fire smouldered in the stone fireplace.

Standing by his chair, she said gently, 'I expect you want to go to your room, don't you?'

'I want that coffee Brett is supposed to be getting. Is the smell of it all I'm to have?' He looked like a spoilt child, Philippa thought, when his favourite toy has been taken away.

Harley said calmly, 'Why not freshen up, Dad, and

I'm sure you must need to go to the bathroom, while Aileen is getting it ready. And I expect Philippa would like to see her room too.'

Taking hold of the chair, he wheeled his father out into the hall, ignoring Clyde's snort, but he had the last word as they passed the kitchen.

'I'll be back, Aileen. Have it ready, and some of your honey cakes too. Come on you two—let's get it over quickly. Real coffee—at last.'

'In moderation, Dad,' Harley reminded him.

They stopped at a door around the corner and Harley waited until Aileen joined them.

'Show Nurse her room and where everything is, will you? And we'll be ready for coffee in five minutes.'

Philippa glanced up at him, a question in her eyes which he understood.

'I'll see to Dad. Five minutes . . .'

'Fine. And thanks,' she said gratefully, while she went with Aileen into the room next to his.

'Oh—this is nice.' Aileen turned, smiling shyly and Philippa, who was beginning to think the housekeeper resented her being there for some reason, now dismissed the idea as ludicrous. She had no real reason to think that; just a feeling because she had avoided looking directly at her. She was probably a naturally shy person and took time to get used to people and this house was suddenly full of them.

'Can I call you Aileen too?' she asked.

'Oh, yes.' A smile curved her lips. 'Do you have all you need?'

'I'm sure I have,' Philippa said happily, looking quickly around the room, mainly furnished in a restful green patterned material with a maroon carpet; the wood, sheer pine, as was the floor surround and furniture. 'And that door?' she asked curiously.

'Your shower and toilet and washbasin. There wasn't room for a bath but there are two main bathrooms just along the corridor.'

Philippa shook her head disbelievingly. 'I didn't expect such luxury way out here. I think I imagined ranch life to be rather primitive.'

'Oh, no. We have good living. Mrs De Winton saw to that. She was a lovely person.'

'I can believe it,' Philippa said soberly, going to wash her hands in the tiny bathroom. There were still some things she didn't quite understand here.

Aileen tactfully disappeared and after tidying her hair, she too went out into the red-carpeted corridor and next door into her patient's room.

It was definitely a masculine room. A desk stood in one corner, the telephone and an angle lamp depicting that he sometimes worked in there. Both bedcover and curtains were tweedy in effect.

Harley was standing with his back to the room, looking out of the window across the huge stretches of grass. Clyde's chair was vacant and she raised questioning eyebrows.

'He's in there,' he said, indicating the tiny bathroom.

'He doesn't manage too well on his own,' she began. 'Perhaps I should . . .'

'He will call if he needs us.'

'Come here . . .' he held out a hand to her. 'Someone should welcome you to Rouen's Creek—properly, Philippa.'

She dared not interpret the expression in his eyes. He reached for her hand and even that was all the signal her body needed to send tremors along her nerves, and as his hand moved up her arm to her shoulder, her neck, and his finger rubbed her cheek gently; while all the time he was coming nearer; she knew a sense of panic. He was going to kiss her. But not here—not now!

'Please go away,' she begged, her eyes slanting up at him luminously, 'now!'

She walked to the door, slim and erect and authoritative because it was her only weapon and she was still in uniform.

For a moment he looked at her reflectively, then, 'Of course—you're quite right, Philippa. Later, perhaps?'

'Oh . . .' she murmured under her breath when he touched her nose teasingly as he went. What did he mean by later? Was he hoping to turn the weekend into something more specialised? Like making her another of his conquests? Was that what this was leading up to? Did she want it to be like that?

Aileen brought her some coffee and a tiny honey cake and Philippa followed her out into the corridor, explaining that her patient was resting but he would probably be up for supper. She knew by the housekeeper's expression that she hadn't realised that he would be quite so restricted in his way of life nor had she accepted that he had almost died during that attack.

'I think there had been others—probably only slight, but he had simply ignored that he was not feeling well.'

'That . . .' Aileen said positively, 'is like him. He only sees what he wants to. But he does look so pale and much thinner.'

'It's early days yet.' How often she had used that phrase to relatives or patients in the past.

Aileen told her that the ambulance driver had left to go back to Prince George.

'Perhaps he wanted his weekend at home,' she suggested.

'More likely that he will be needed on duty,' Philippa told her. 'It's a very busy hospital and everyone works full out. Especially now the tourists are coming through. What time is supper?'

'Seven-thirty, Dr Harley said.'

'Right. I'll be through by then and have time to get Mr De Winton up without rushing.'

'Dr Harley said to lay for four and you're to eat in the dining-room—they often have meals in the kitchen, Mr De Winton likes that. But tonight is kind of special, isn't it?' Her voice was soft and gentle and Philippa could understand why Clyde liked having her around his home.

There was something rather restful about her. But there were also hidden depths—she felt sure of that.

Looking at the other doors leading from the corridor she wondered idly which room was Harley's. It would be a little strange knowing that he was sleeping somewhere quite near.

As if in answer to her thoughts as she came back from checking his father, he came along the corridor.

'Is he okay?'

'Yes. Just got a little too excited, I think,' she said softly.

Raising his eyebrows, he murmured huskily, 'You have that effect upon me as well . . .' and before she knew it he had put his hand at the back of her neck and pulled her towards him, finding her mouth and probing until she swayed unresistingly even nearer to the lean body moulded so closely to her own.

When he let her go she took a step backwards, her breath coming unevenly as she attempted to cover her flushed face with her hands.

'I was right,' he said softly, a pleased smile playing around his mouth now. 'You couldn't not respond—when I want you so much. Surely you knew?'

'How—could I?' she whispered.

He kissed the tip of her nose. 'Well—you do now. But as you reminded me, there's a time and place—under the present circumstances,' and she saw his eyes go to the open door of the room where Clyde was asleep. 'And I have to change and go round the place with Brett. I guess he's still out there waiting for me—so, later for us, my sweet.'

He bent to kiss her mouth fleetingly. 'That's just to go on with.' And as he opened the door of the room opposite, turned and gave her such a warmly intimate look, making all her senses respond yet again, that she leaned for a moment against the door frame for support.

She hadn't been able to resist when Harley kissed her. She hadn't even wanted to. It was happening all over again, only Nick had never evoked this depth of wanting in her body. She hadn't felt this drowning sensation when he looked at her either. His deeply disturbing gaze could certainly throw her into a new world of uncertainty which undermined her own resolutions while all the time her body was revelling in the wonder of it all.

She had wanted to hold him so close that he became a part of her, so desperately, just a little time ago. Even now, she was aware that only a pine door separated them. It would be that way for the next two nights—just a door between her and the ecstasy of loving she would find in his arms.

But her own moral discipline was very strong and told her there were more barriers than just a door between them. She was here in her profession as nurse to his father and on duty at night as well as by day for as long as she stayed. And there was no way she could forget that.

She heard a car speeding up to the door, its tyres crunching on the gravel. A car door slammed. Someone ran up the wooden steps—a girl's voice rang through the wood-built house.

'Aileen—where's Dr Harley? In his room? Okay—
no, I'll go through. I think I know the way—don't you?'

Philippa, trying to accept something new, heard the
knowing laugh which accompanied her last words but
she was already inside Clyde's room, hearing him groan
restlessly as his sleep was disturbed suddenly by the
noise, checking that he was all right. He seemed to be,
except for a few twitches as he convulsively clutched the
duvet cover.

Harley had opened his door when he heard the foot-
steps coming nearer and it was as well no one heard the
expletive he muttered under his breath.

He emerged wearing a casual shirt and brown cords
now and as the girl reached him she threw herself into his
arms, bringing his head down to hers, kissing him hard.

'Darling—why didn't I know you were coming this
weekend?'

'Hi, Rachel,' Harley said quietly. 'I didn't have time
to call you. So, how did you know I was here?'

'I saw the car from the top of the hill. My horse was
lame and I was walking him back. Saw you come out of
the trees. Was that an ambulance behind?'

Harley answered briefly. 'Yes. But you came round by
the road—why not across the lake?'

'Damned outboard motor wouldn't start,' she told
him crossly. Then, changing her tone she said sexily,
'Oh—honey—it's so good to see you—I've missed
you.'

'Come along to the lounge—Dad's asleep,' Harley
said crisply, looking over his shoulder, but he didn't see
Philippa standing just inside the door of Clyde's room,
both hands pressed to her trembling mouth while waves
of anger spread through her. Anger and disappointment
both. The first at herself for being taken in by him so
simply and the second because of the great build up of

hopes, of her trust that here at last was a man who would not let her down—it couldn't happen again—that kind of deception. Yet it had. For no one had told her about Rachel. Yes—Clyde had. What was it he had said that day in his room? *'You'll be cutting Rachel out if he's that interested.'*

'Oh . . .' Well—there was still Rachel and she had been stupid not to have realised there must be someone like her in his life.

Glancing at her watch she remembered Clyde's pills. He should have them at six. It was past that already and she was annoyed that she had let this happen. Also, her bag was still in the hall, another unusual thing for her to be slack about, because all of his medications were inside it, except for those he carried on his person for just such an angina attack as one he had had earlier.

She went quickly along the red carpet and into the hall to where she had put her bag. It was still there on the chair.

Through the open doorway she saw Harley talking to Rachel, standing beside a red sports car, vivid against the green of the flowing lawns stretching to the hills beyond. Her heart seemed to contract because of the girl's devastating looks. She could never hope to hold a candle to the way she looked. Her raven-black hair fell over her shoulders, glossy and rippling. She was wearing a flame blouse open at the front and cream culottes, worn too with the same flair; and her superb figure was one of voluptuous enticement as she leaned towards Harley, laughing up into his face.

He was regarding her with thoughtful amusement and Philippa would have given much to know what his thoughts were just then. Nevertheless, he took her with him as he walked over to where Brett was standing looking at the horses in the corral.

Philippa turned and went silently back to her patient, unaware that the housekeeper, seeing her from the kitchen and about to ask her a question about Mr Clyde's diet, changed her mind, deciding to wait until later when she saw the look of dejection, even pain, on the girl's face.

When Clyde was ready Philippa took him along the corridor in his chair. Harley and Brett were already there, both wearing suits in his honour tonight. And sitting with her legs crossed in an armchair by the window was Rachel.

'Is this a party?' Clyde joked—seeing they all had glasses in their hands. 'Can anyone join in? Hullo there—Rachel. I didn't know you were here.'

'Well—you see that I am, Mr De Winton. I guess you're much better—and—who is this?'

Her eyes slid over the girl in nurse's uniform almost insolently, certainly critically; but she couldn't find much fault with a purple-belted white dress and flat white shoes, nor with the diminutive cap perched on top of the shining hair pinned back in the style of someone's maiden aunt.

'This is Nurse Croft,' Harley said, enjoying the moment immensely as he got up and went to help her in with the chair. Then when Clyde was settled in his own armchair and she had pushed it to one side, Philippa gratefully accepted her dry Martini from him, wondering if their fingers had touched by chance or design.

'Do I get a Scotch?' Clyde was asking.

'Not yet. Maybe in a week or so,' Harley answered.

'But we're having champagne tonight, aren't we?'

'No—just wine. You can have a little of that.'

Clyde tossed an appealing glance across the room at Philippa who smiled back, very conscious that the other girl was watching her over the rim of her glass, sensing a new situation here at the ranch; one she hadn't previously encountered.

Brett's arrival made conversation somewhat easier because they discussed cattle and the winter's toll. It had been rather a bad one and because her father was also a rancher across on the other side of the lake, Rachel joined in knowledgeably and now it was Philippa's turn to feel a bit outside things.

There was one embarrassing moment, however. When Aileen came to announce that supper was ready, she said in her soft voice,

'Oh—I didn't know that there was an extra place needed. I've only laid for four. I'll see to it.'

'Well,' Rachel broke in. 'We are only four surely?'

'No,' Harley said in his decisive tone, 'we are five. That is, if you intend staying too, Rachel.'

'I can eat in the kitchen,' Philippa said quickly, 'that way Aileen won't have to change anything.'

'I want you with me.' Clyde was in control now. 'Lay another place, Aileen.'

Rachel covered her slight embarrassment with a request for another drink. 'You're slipping, darling,' she murmured as Harley took her proffered glass. 'You usually know when I want another one.'

Clyde looked at Philippa sitting on a velvet pouffe near him. 'Do you like my home? Is it what you expected after all my going on about it?'

'I love it. What I've seen already. Especially this room. It's a room to relax in.'

'It's the home Greta and I made together. So much of her is here . . .'

Harley knew the signs of emotion which are usually part of the aftermath of a severe heart attack and said he'd decided to do some fishing next day.

'Oh—I thought we might spend it together,' Rachel

began, just as Aileen came back.

'I've put another place,' she said and as Philippa pushed Clyde into the dining-room she had a very distinct feeling of an underlying constraint between the others before Brett joined them, taking care of the wine because Harley and Rachel were still talking in the room they had left.

CHAPTER EIGHT

WHEN Clyde announced, half-way through eating the delicious blueberry pie which Aileen had made specially, that he wanted to go back to his room, it was quite a relief for Philippa who pushed back her chair at once.

'Enough is enough,' he said, looking all in, as his keen eyes scanned the faces around the table. 'I'm sorry to have to drag you away . . .' he ended, looking up at her apologetically.

'It doesn't matter at all.'

Harley was already coming to help her get him into his wheelchair.

'Are you feeling okay, Dad?'

'Oh, sure. Just a bit tired. Guess I haven't sat up on an ordinary day chair for this long—takes a bit of getting used to. Just—carry on. My nurse won't mind, will you?'

'Of course not,' she answered at once. 'It's been quite a day for you . . .' and they all saw his grateful glance up into her face.

'Finish your meal,' he commanded as Philippa wheeled him out into the corridor.

But Harley was right behind them when they reached his room and waited while Philippa helped him into his pyjamas and into bed before making a quick check to make quite sure there were no complication signals.

'I'm okay,' Clyde confided when he was through. 'I just couldn't take any more of Rachel's chatter. She's a bit high tonight, isn't she?'

'She does go on a bit,' Harley agreed looking at the

back of Philippa's head, while she folded Clyde's clothes and put the rest on hangers.

'I don't think she stopped talking once,' Clyde remarked drily. 'Who asked her to stay anyway? Tonight of all nights—my head is still full of her voice.'

'She probably thought we needed a bit of livening up, conversation-wise; filling you in with all the gossip while you've been away.'

'I can do without it.'

'Well, it's always a bit traumatic making the transition from hospital to a home environment,' Harley said quietly, 'more especially when you're still convalescent. I expect she didn't understand that.'

'Then someone should tell her. She's piqued over something, Harley, and it shows,' his father said solidly, 'and I can guess what it is. Better go back or she'll be clap-trapping the pants off Brett.'

Philippa saw Harley's lips twitch but he kept a straight face as he walked to turn off the main light, leaving just the bedside lamp which plunged the room into a soft glow. 'I'll look in again later, Dad, but I shall probably go down to the lodge during the evening.'

'Okay.'

Philippa, who had gone across the corridor to her room with her medical bag, came out again as Harley left his father's room.

He barred her way, taking hold of her arm with his other hand spread behind her shoulder, while he regarded her solemnly. 'Philippa—trust me, can't you? It isn't the way it appears on the surface, you know.'

'No—I don't know. Neither do I understand what you're trying to say.'

'I think you do. It's important to me that you do.'

'Well—not to me. Not any more,' she said icily, 'and if you don't mind—I'd like to get back to my patient.'

'I'm not unaware of the kind of ordeal you were subjected to at dinner,' he said gently, lifting her chin to look into her eyes, 'and I apologise . . .'

'Then you might have done something about it,' she returned coldly. 'In future, unless we're alone, I shall eat in the kitchen with Aileen, where it seems your guest expected me to be.'

'You're being childish—and I didn't think you could be.'

'I have every reason . . .'

'You will eat with Father, of course.' He was angry now. 'It's what he wants that matters. It's why you are here, to stay with him, especially at meal times.'

'You don't need to remind me what my duties are, Dr De Winton. And, as you said—that is why I am here. Please let me pass.'

A combination of disappointment and disillusion after what had happened between them earlier, Rachel's appearance and the suppression of any recognition of the hidden snide remarks at dinner, had really upset her. There were tears at the back of her eyes which she refused to let him see, so she forcibly pushed him aside and went into his father's room.

Although he was rather pale, he was nevertheless very much in command and told her to sit down. 'I want to talk to you.'

'You—didn't hear all that, did you?'

'Enough. I want you to do something.'

'Of course. What is it?'

'Go to the kitchen and bring back the coffee we didn't have.'

'You're incorrigible. And I wish you wouldn't. It's not like hospital coffee. It's too stimulating.'

'Thank God it's not. And I need stimulating. So do you. Just give me those cattle magazines on the table to look at while you're gone. And bring Greta's picture over here where I can see it.'

At least I know where I stand with him, she thought, feeling a heaviness somewhere in her heart which wasn't there before dinner, as she went through to the kitchen. A child's treble voice mingled with the dishwashing as Aileen cleared up after the meal· and the smell of smouldering wood in the lounge caught her nostrils as she passed the door.

Aileen, working methodically as she put everything away in its place, was answering the questions of a small girl of seven or eight who was perched on a stool at the table, drawing. She was an exact replica of her mother and had the same slow smile which completely transformed her face when Philippa smiled in her normally friendly fashion and said, 'Hullo . . .'

'It must seem very strange for you to have a nurse around the place,' she mused, looking at Aileen.

'Yes. But it's nice to have another woman, too.'

'Oh—I hadn't thought of it in that way. Mr De Winton would like some coffee,' she explained. 'Can I make it?'

'There is always some keeping hot,' Aileen told her. 'Just come and help yourself whenever you like. There is orange juice too in the fridge if I shouldn't be around in the morning early. I get Maura off to school before I prepare breakfast.'

'I see. Thanks. And what a lovely name you have, Maura.'

The child flushed with pleasure. Children were soon on to Philippa's wavelength. She hadn't been a very popular nurse on the paediatric wards without leaving her mark. Confidence in one's nurse was everything.

Aileen was taking two Wedgwood cups from the cupboard, a tall coffee-pot and cream and sugar containers to match.

'Oh—no cream for either of us. And only skimmed milk for Mr De Winton when he does have it. I'll bring his sheet along. He is on a low cholesterol, low fat diet for a time at least.'

Aileen grimaced. 'He won't like that.'

'He's more or less used to it now, I think. Actually, he's been a very co-operative patient.'

'You didn't finish your sweet at dinner,' she was reminded. 'Would you like some now?'

'Oh—no. But thank you for thinking of it. Mr De Winton was a little tired and needed to rest.'

'I'm not surprised,' Aileen said with some feeling, at which her small daughter raised her eyes to her mother's face wonderingly.

Carrying the tray, Philippa felt that she and the house-keeper were going to understand each other very well. But then, no one suspected that she was deeply unhappy because of what had happened between Harley and herself. She hadn't been prepared for it, that angry exchange of words with the last man in the world she had wanted to be angry with.

It left such aching disappointment but what had she expected? That he was seriously in love with her? That his kisses were anything but just a sexual attraction of that moment? And she had fallen for it. Well—not any more. But he knew that now, of course.

Clyde was well aware that his coffee was weakened but he made no comment, seeming to enjoy it as he watched her over the top of his cup.

'When you take the tray back, why don't you get some air—take a walk around for half an hour or so? I'm okay. It's still light out there.'

'Perhaps . . .' she hedged.

They both heard the noisy revving up of a car engine as the red car sped away down the long drive and she couldn't help wondering if Harley had gone too.

'I'm off on a tour of inspection tomorrow morning,' Clyde announced. 'You're going to push me around the stables and feed-barns and I'll give you a running commentary. Okay?'

'Okay,' she told him, laughingly. 'Now—do you mind if I call my sister in Edmonton? I'll pay, of course. It could be quite a few dollars.'

'You'll do nothing of the kind. Just go ahead.'

'Thanks. You do have everything you want, don't you? And, please—don't try to get out of bed unless someone is here.'

'Sure. You're the nurse.'

'And you're the boss. Is that what you're saying?'

'You're dead right it is. And tomorrow, they'll all know I'm back.'

Emma was out but Oliver sounded quite concerned, even relieved, and certainly interested when she explained exactly where the ranch was situated.

'Rouen's Creek is on the map. I know where you are now. Still out in the sticks but good for the summer months. Is—everything else okay?'

'Everything,' she said, taking an easy way out of more explanations but wondering if he had detected a certain note in her voice. 'Here is the number to ring if you want to get to me. If you call England, tell them I'm writing, will you?'

'Sure. Danny's here and wants a word.'

'Hullo—Danny.'

'Hi. I'll be quite glad when you come back to Edmonton,' he told her wistfully.

'Really? How nice to think you're missing me. I'll be back some time. Lots of love to Mum. Be good.'

'Okay. Are there any other little guys where you are?'

'No. One little girl—that's all.'

'Ugh. Goodbye now. Come back soon.'

The phone call did something to revive her jaded spirits as she wandered out on to the veranda. Until she remembered that day on the lake when she first saw Harley—and again she wished fervently that tonight hadn't happened.

If only she had kept the whole thing in perspective. He was a surgeon—she knew that—and she a visiting nurse. So when had the situation changed to the more basic one of just a man and woman with natural instincts mounting so fast? On the train? Perhaps. She had certainly been aware of him then, especially in that ridiculously short robe. But it was when he kissed her that first night at Prince George. That was when all her pulses leapt to meet his. His hand on her neck. She reached to touch the spot, shivering at the memory, jumping violently when Brett's voice came from a chair at the back of the veranda.

'If you're cold, you should get a coat or go back inside. Nights can be treacherous up here.'

He uncoiled himself and stood up, regarding her somewhat shyly. 'I guess Father's asleep.'

'Not when I left. He's reading actually.'

'He's feeling better then?'

'Yes. I'd say so. The trauma of the day since early morning and the excitement after the journey was all a bit much.'

'I'll go in and see him.'

'He'd like that,' she smiled gratefully.

'If you're looking for Harley, he's gone down to the lodge.'

She looked surprised. Was she unknowingly looking for him?

So he hadn't gone home with Rachel after all.

'Where and what is the lodge?' she asked, evading the question.

'It belongs to Harley. It is one of the early-built log houses and he's doing some upgrading on it. He mainly uses it for a fishing lodge. It's right down there by the lakeside; you can't see it from here, just beyond the trees. Yes—you can just see the lake shore if you look behind the boathouse.'

Philippa followed the direction which he had indicated and caught a glimpse of red through the trees. It had to be Rachel's car. Brett too had seen it now.

'Is it habitable? The cabin?' she asked carefully.

'Oh, sure. I guess Harley's lit the fire to air it out after the winter. It's furnished, but roughly. Comfortable enough though. He likes to go there when he needs a bit of peace after Prince George. It's certainly peaceful, by the lake. Maybe he'll take you to see the work he's done on it.'

'Yes,' she said through taut lips, 'perhaps he will. But you're right—one does need a coat at night, it's quite chilly. I'll be in my room if you want me and once Mr De Winton is settled I'll have a shower and an early night too. I'll leave my door open so that I shall hear if he calls.'

'Right. Just ask Aileen if you want anything. Her room is just at the end of the passage by the kitchen.'

She flashed him a grateful smile. 'Thanks.'

And she never knew that after she had gone in, Brett stood for a full three minutes looking out over the dusky valley to where a thin spiral of smoke rose upwards from Harley's chimney. He didn't need to be told that Rachel was still there too. It was usual for her to be around when he came to Rouen's Creek. He wouldn't have expected her not to be; except that this time, there was a difference. And Harley was probably having a hard time explaining why.

It was just eleven-thirty when Philippa, fresh from her shower, went in to check Clyde before getting into bed herself. She was completely organised now, knowing where everything she might need in a hurry was, in readiness. Her patient's pulse and BP was just a little erratic but she wasn't unduly worried. It was all consistent with the upheaval and changed diet; and domicile.

She could hear muffled music coming from the lounge, quite some way from the bedrooms, and Harley's door was still ajar. The house was otherwise quiet.

She needn't have worried about her feelings—or his—with his room so close and his door a few steps from hers, she thought wistfully. It would never arise now.

Drawing back the curtains from the window, she gazed at an errant moon high in the heavens, sailing into the moving clouds. Outside was almost total blackness. No street lights as at Prince George—no passing cars, no hub of a town's night life, no neon signs blasting overhead. Silence . . . But as she turned away, even that was broken by the shrill call of a bird.

Then there were sounds of activity from the men's quarters and a shaft of light, a girl's subdued laughter. Probably the married ones. They must, she supposed, make their own pleasures out here so far from a town. But tonight she envied them their laughter and whatever caused it. It only succeeded in making her feel even more lonely.

Sleep evaded her. Her mind refused to exclude those thoughts clamouring to come to the surface and be examined. And now she was living again every moment in Harley's arms. His aloofness, arrogance, call it what she liked, all disappeared in the evidence that he wanted her. She fired him, holding her so close to his lean body that she was aware of all its contours, straining for closer contact with her own. She wanted it to go on—until . . .

No . . . This was sheer stupidity, she groaned, as she sat up against her pillows and switched on her bedside light. What was she hoping to gain from remembering his searching kiss, long and blissful—making her ache with longing. Oh, the joy of it, leaving them breathless after. And shaken. And the look in his eyes—that was real enough. And the gentleness of his hands behind her head as he drew her close to his mouth. He couldn't have been just playing around then. Yet, all the time, he knew there was Rachel.

And that relationship was nothing new, she told herself bitterly. She was too possessive—and wanted Philippa to be aware of it. So they had gone off together and he was still not back. Perhaps he didn't intend to sleep here tonight. Well—that was all she needed to know, surely.

She flung back the covers, partly to relieve her troubled mind and also because she thought she heard a sound from Clyde's room. It would be just like him to try to reach his small bathroom without disturbing her, and he just might not be fully awake and could fall. Pulling on her dressing-gown, she padded on bare feet to make sure.

He had knocked Greta's photo over as he tried to find the light switch, not really awake.

'I think,' she said firmly, 'we should go back to the same procedure you used in hospital—just for a time. I would rather you didn't get out of bed on your own.'

He grunted, finding it difficult to breathe too well. Even this exertion was proving exhausting. He knew this too and didn't waste his energy by protesting.

Waiting until he was settled once more, she crept back to her room. Everyone now seemed to be asleep, the house silent. Only she was fruitlessly throwing away her sleeping hours in useless heart searching and aching longing.

Pushing her pillow under her cheek resignedly, the way she liked to sleep, she heard nothing then until morning. Nor did she know that Harley returned in the early hours, closing his door very quietly so as not to disturb her. But the low light from the corridor shining into her room had been just enough for him to see her fair hair spread over the pillow and her face in repose like that of a child, while her bare arm had been flung outstretched. He wanted to creep in and put it under the covers but she might waken and he couldn't risk that. Not tonight.

Philippa, waking around seven, got up, pulled on her gown and saw his closed door. A kind of hot anger rippled through her, vying with the disappointment of yesterday. An unjustified anger, she thought, because he was back, but an emotion she couldn't help.

Clyde was still asleep and although there were signs of activity coming from outside and the sound of hoofs as someone rode past the window, no one else in the house seemed to be up. She wondered idly where Brett's room was. There were two other doors, other than the bathrooms. He probably had one of them.

The kitchen was pleasantly cool this morning as she took the orange juice from the fridge. Someone else had obviously done the same thing; an empty glass stood by an enormous coffee mug, the mug still warm. Brett, of course.

Standing at the window drinking her juice, she watched as he led a horse already saddled from the stable yard, swinging up into the saddle looking muscular and fit, his stetson hat at the back of his head, while he held the reins lightly and turned his horse before breaking into a canter. He has such a strong face, she thought, watching man and horse disappear into the trees. Why can't I fall in love with someone like that? Does it have to be a doctor each time? Why not a rancher, or anyone else?

Her sigh came from deep down within her taut body and the man standing nonchalantly in the doorway was fully aware of her tensions as he came further into the kitchen, wearing the same diminutive towelling robe he had worn on the train. His feet, like hers, were bare.

She had swung round at his approach and she saw at once that his eyes ran over her, down to her toes and back to the soft golden hair cascading almost to her shoulders, and it did nothing to improve her mood towards him as she put down her empty glass and turned to leave.

His hand detained her. 'We really must stop meeting like this,' he said softly, the intonations in his voice leaving her in no doubt that he intended to behave as if nothing had happened between Rachel's arrival and now. Did he really think she would fill in when she was absent?

'Did you sleep well?' he went on, removing his hand from her arm.

She nodded, feeling utterly miserable as his dark eyes probed hers indolently, but determined now that he shouldn't see how much he was disturbing her.

'Father too?'

'He seems to have had quite a good night.'

'Yes. He was quite happy when I looked in on him.'

'Excuse me. I must get dressed.' She met his eyes belligerently and saw his expression change.

'I see. No chance to explain, is that it?'

'You have no need to explain anything to me,' she retorted, her lips moulding into a firm line, mainly to stop them quivering. Her chin rose defiantly. 'Just don't think I'm interested in becoming another of your conquests. I'm here and I'll stay until Mr De Winton is well enough for me to leave, and that's the end of it.'

He spun round just as he had been about to pour orange juice into a glass. His eyes narrowed. She had never seen him quite so angry. 'Then I suggest you do just that,' he said icily.

Well—she had asked for it, Philippa kept reminding herself as she got into her uniform and bent her head to tie the white laces of her shoes which she now associated with the rest of it. Then, brushing her hair furiously, she twisted it into a knot on top of her head and jammed on her cap, savagely venting some of her anger on herself, for wasn't she partly to blame for what had happened just now? Couldn't she have managed the whole thing better than that? Either by ignoring it, when he would have realised why, and certainly by not losing her cool.

Fortunately she wouldn't have to see him after tomorrow and when he drove down again to see his father she just might be more in control.

Her mood softened when she saw that her patient was awake and enjoying the fact of being in his own room.

She stood looking down at him while she waited for him to swallow his tablets. Then she put her fingers over his pulse and lifted the watch on her breast to monitor the beats. It was faster than of late and she decided to check his blood pressure, finding it raised again.

'No aches or pains?' she asked easily, while she filled in her report, making her voice deliberately casual.

'Yes . . .' he admitted, 'just a twinge or two here. I—didn't call you.'

'Why? That's what I'm here for. Probably the result of

yesterday's journey and excitement. What about breakfast in bed?'

'Okay. Just toast.'

'Cereal and toast, at least. Are you sure you wouldn't like something more?'

He shook his head, looking remote. 'Do you know Philippa—before—all this—I'd have ham and eggs every day and when we were rounding up, a thick beefsteak.' He shook his head. 'I'm not the man I was—that's for sure. The trouble is, I don't know what I can expect in the future, either. Everyone seems to evade the issue—and now—even you. I think I'm on the right road—then—this.'

'That pain—it was worse than you told me, wasn't it?' She thought that might account for the dampness of his skin as he nodded slowly.

'Did you take one of your tablets?'

'Couldn't reach 'em. I just tried breathing deep as I could and kept still for a bit. This is just between us—remember.'

'Well—rest now and no getting up until lunchtime.'

'I said I'd look around the place this morning. Brett thinks . . .'

'This afternoon should do just as well,' she told him firmly, 'and you'll probably enjoy it a lot better than. I'll go and see about breakfast.'

But it was to Harley she went first, finding him coming from one of the bathrooms, his hair damply clinging to his head and the clean smell of soap and aftershave reminding her sharply of that night on the train.

'I was looking for you . . .' she began, and saw his eyes express concern as they looked down into hers.

'Is something wrong?'

'I'm—not too happy about your father this morning,' she said quietly, going on to tell him why and only then realising that he was standing there shivering in the cold air which came right through the house from the huge door—which seemed always to be open, she discovered in the next weeks.

'I'll come and see him,' he said briefly, passing her and going into his room.

Aileen was in the kitchen where breakfast had been laid, after seeing her child off to school, one of the ranch hands having driven her down to pick up the rumbling old bus which came around the outlying districts.

'Did the boss have a good night?' she asked conversationally.

'Quite good. He's having the morning in bed so I'll take his tray along.'

She busied herself with getting it ready and was just on her way when Brett appeared, coming in through a back door, his boots muddied and wearing only a checked shirt and jeans.

'Hi, there . . .'

'Good morning.'

'What's this? Not breakfast in bed surely?'

She nodded.

'And he's accepting it?'

'He's tired,' she told him, 'and he doesn't really have much choice. He does have to take things very slowly. I expect you'll have to help in that. You see, he's going to pretend that he's stronger than he is and especially in front of his men.'

'So—today's inspection is out?'

'Perhaps after lunch. It might do him good.'

'Okay. Thanks.'

She felt so completely at ease with this tall, broad-shouldered rancher with the shy, thoughtful eyes. And she had a strong feeling that he saw more than people realised.

Harley, wearing a casual cream summer sweater and cotton pants, was talking to his father.

'I suggest,' he was saying easily, 'that you do as your nurse suggests and rest up this morning and this afternoon we'll all go on a tour around the ranch. I'm off down to the lodge. Brett is sending Tom down to put up a few shelves for me. And I have to get the water flow organised; the shower down there doesn't have enough power.'

'You need your own generator.'

'I know. That lake water needs a lot of purifying before it's fit for drinking purposes. There's a lot to be done yet—but I'm in no hurry. Meanwhile, I'll go and eat while you do the same, and—just slow up a bit—eh?'

Philippa saw him press his father's shoulder affectionately. Then his eyes met hers quite deliberately. 'Why don't you come and have breakfast too and leave him to enjoy his quietly? I'm sure he would prefer that.'

'You're right. I would. And when the mail comes, tell Brett I want it brought in here and not to the office. I'm back now and running this ranch. We'll—go through it together. Don't forget.'

'Okay,' his son promised resignedly before holding the door open for Philippa to go through.

'You'll have to get used to leaving him sometimes,' he told her as they walked together along the corridor. 'You can't watch him for twenty-four hours out of twenty-four. You know as well as I that there isn't going to be any great improvement. His heart is coping but only just. I think we have to accept the fact that complications are always possible and other than medication there is very little else to do for him. As much as possible, let him live as near normal a life as he'll allow. Not an easy thing for you, Philippa,' he said, stopping now to face her. 'Only someone as special as you would attempt it. Brett and I are—grateful. But you know how I feel about you. I'm just sorry things have gone wrong the way they have between us—I'd hoped—oh—maybe it's for the best. Come and have breakfast. Brett will be curious to know what's been going on.'

He hadn't given her a chance to comment.

But as they all three talked around the table a much happier atmosphere prevailed and she realised how hungry she was.

'You're going back tomorrow?' Brett asked him.

Harley nodded. 'I must. I'm doing Dale Bonek's laminectomy and fusion on Monday. He's flying up tomorrow from Jasper, I hope. In fact, I've quite a hefty list. I shall drive back early evening. Probably have a word with Dr Gurnett. He may call you . . .' He spoke to Philippa now. 'In any case, don't hesitate to call me if you're worried. You know the procedure. Now—I'm off to do a spot of fishing. I caught three trout last night but when it came to around three I just left the net out and came back.'

'You were fishing?' Philippa murmured in a very small voice.

'That's right. Where did you think I was?'

CHAPTER NINE

PHILIPPA dragged her eyes from the half-amused expression in his, darkly teasing—as if to say 'So what?'

She couldn't help the flood of relief passing through her mind and body as the tension lifted, to disappear amazingly from her taut muscles. Never had ham and eggs tasted so good as she attacked them healthily, avoiding looking up again and letting Brett and Harley's conversation simply drift over her head while they talked ranch business.

Then Brett was saying, 'I guess Dad forgot we don't get mail on Saturdays. Unless it's urgent, then we collect. Maybe it's as well if he has a quiet weekend. He gets so uptight about everything to do with the ranch. And he has no need—I've ironed out most of the problems which leaves just day-to-day decisions. But the old man was slipping a bit, Harley. Guess he hadn't felt too well for some time. I should have seen this coming.'

'You mean, I should . . .' Harley said vehemently. At which Philippa looked across the table at his set face. 'But would it have made any difference? Would he have slowed up? I doubt it. But keep any problems off his back,' he advised, 'as much as he'll let you, Brett. Philippa is a good ally. She can twist him round her little finger.'

'I wouldn't say that.'

Both men were watching her now, each in his different way, with her fresh, healthy skin and huge blue eyes under the fair silkiness of hair, neatly coiled off her neck. There was even something in Brett's face which disconcerted her too, so she got up from the table and said quietly,

'I'll do whatever I can, you know that.'

She heard their mumbled 'Thanks . . .' but was half out of the door by that time, leaving them to talk while she went along to collect Clyde's tray.

It was a lovely day with a marked new warmth in the sun and a vividly blue sky, with just a few high wispy cotton-wool clouds, a perfect backcloth for the tall dark spruce edging the ranch compound.

Sliding back the double glazed windows, she breathed in the clear freshness of mountain air, tasting vaguely of clover blossom.

'Lovely,' she said happily. 'I suppose the mesh is to keep out mosquitoes?'

'Yes. They're lethal,' Clyde commented from his pillow where he too could see the lovely mistiness over the meadows. And putting down yesterday's news-papers, gave her a boyish grin, 'I'll be making my trip outside then this morning. It's time the men knew the boss is around again.'

'Yes. I'm looking forward to looking round too. How many permanent staff do you have?'

'Ranch hands? Well—there's my foreman, Larry. Wilf and Bart look to the horse stock and Joe and Tooter, good cattlemen both of 'em. We take on drovers if we need 'em—come round-up time—and I've done a good day's work myself until this happened. Brett's well able to run this place when I can't. And that's not yet. I'll be back in that saddle if it's the last thing I do.'

She couldn't say anything to dishearten him but it could be just that—the effort too much for his damaged heart muscles.

Later, when she was pushing his chair around the ranch yard, she met most of the men. And Jamie,

Larry's wife. Log cabins stood under the trees, away from each other, and the door of the foreman's stood open and Philippa saw how comfortable the interior looked with brightly-coloured scatter cushions and rugs on a solid wood floor.

Brett came to help her over the grassy tufts because Clyde was anxious that she should see for herself and it was he who extolled their comforts. 'Each has a shower and inside toilet,' he said. 'A good-sized kitchen too—and bedroom. That's the lounge, as you see.'

Larry came up to say that his wife was going to the stores. 'If there's anything you want brought back. I believe Aileen is going with her, and Maura. She and our little guy are great friends. And you know what it's like when the women get near a store.'

'Okay. We'll press on,' Clyde interrupted. 'I want to see how much winter feed we've got left.'

'I told you about that,' Brett reminded him.

'So? I guess I can look at my own feed store if I decide to.'

He was finding it tiring and a somewhat emotional experience, Philippa knew, and his irritability only natural. She saw how emotional he became when his dun-coloured horse was led out of his stable to him, swishing his black tail as he pawed the ground impatiently.

'Saddle him up,' Clyde ordered. 'One of you guys give him a good gallop. Keep him exercised. I'll be up there myself soon. Get that temper out of his eyes.'

There were calves too, whose mothers were already back with the herd; and barns to inspect and be put in the picture and half an hour later he looked up at Brett, seeming enormous with his broad shoulders, as he took over from Philippa.

'Take me back—that's enough for one day, I guess, boy.'

Philippa appreciated what the older rancher must be feeling, as Brett's boots crunched over the gravel towards the house. His frustration must be immense. Not to be able to get on his horse and ride out over the ranges; inspect his cattle as he was used to doing. Small wonder that he kept silent until he was back on the veranda, his face drawn from the sheer effort of concealing his feelings from the others.

'Get me a cold beer, Brett. I'll sit here for a while,' he said soberly, while Philippa sat down on a three-legged stool near to him. 'And you can take some time off.'

She looked up at him in surprise. 'Me?'

'There's no one else around. Go for a walk—anything—you're entitled to some time to yourself. Don't you have a union or anything?'

She shook her head laughingly. 'No—I'm specialling you—or didn't you know that?'

'Well—just take off. There are enough of those guys around to give a hand if I need anything. And I mean that.'

She bent to adjust his chair, pulling out the support for his legs from under it, not hearing Brett until he was beside them, carrying two cans of beer.

'I've told her to take a couple of hours off,' Clyde said testily, while her eyes sought reassurance from Brett. 'I'm not an invalid incapable of doing for myself. The girl needs some free time on a day like this.'

'I agree,' he said easily. 'I'll stay around—maybe Harley will be back later. If you feel like a walk—just go down the path through the trees and you'll come out on to the lakeside.'

'Thanks,' she told him gratefully. 'It would be nice.'

She changed swiftly into pale blue cotton slacks and a short sleeved cotton blouse to match and flat shoes because she didn't know what might lie underfoot among the trees. Clyde was dozing and didn't see her go and Brett had drawn up a chair, busy with paperwork on the table in front of him, just lifting his hand to her as she passed and because she didn't look round, she never knew that his eyes followed his father's nurse as she went towards the path into the trees, through which she had already caught sight of the glistening water.

It led her right on to the lake shore and one of the most beautiful settings she had ever seen. The trees, green and thick with new leaves, dipped their branches in the blue waters of the creek, a perfect contrast to the blue-grey of the mountains, rising against the flowing skyline. A few broken branches lay around on the shore, flotsam from the storms of winter. Two Herefords grazed on the grassy tufts near the trees, obviously separated from the rest of the herd. This was the start of the huge lake which stretched wide and endless across to the shore on the other side and for miles away into the far country where the rocks reached higher until they too joined the mountain range.

Across the lake she could see a boathouse; small boats moored to it and a few scattered houses up in the hills. Turning, she walked along the pebble shore enjoying the peace of it all. She could imagine Indians living here in the creek, which Harley said they had, fishing for food, camp-fires in the night. Tents under the trees there.

The water looked so cool and clear she had an urge to slip off her shoes and put her feet into it; among the pebbles at the bottom where small fish darted tantalisingly through it, but she resisted because, as she veered around a bend, she saw through a clearing a log cabin which must belong to Harley. And there was a small boathouse and a staging, with his boat tied up.

Suddenly, the memory of that first meeting was back in her mind. She couldn't have known then where it was going to lead. Right up here in British Columbia. And instead of her heart recovering from Nick, she was nursing a more recent bruising from Dr De Winton.

Kicking a pebble rebelliously, she told herself, 'You're too vulnerable by far . . .' and jumped violently when Harley's voice came from a few feet behind her.

'I wouldn't have thought so . . .' he said thoughtfully.

She spun round. He was standing against a tree trunk, watching her, a grin appearing when he saw her confusion.

'Did I . . . ?'

'You did. I certainly wasn't expecting to see you down here. What happened?'

'Your father insisted I took some time off, that's all. So Brett offered to stay with him.'

'Don't tell me that you came looking for me,' he teased.

'Of course not. I thought you were with your . . .'

'Rachel?'

She nodded, wishing he wouldn't stare at her so intently. He only ever did this when he was sure they were alone. It was like being undressed, stripped bare of whatever protection she was hiding behind.

'Yes. Rachel. Who else?'

'Now why should you think that there is anything unusual between Rachel and me?'

'I didn't say—unusual. Besides—she rather gives that impression, doesn't she?'

Ignoring her question, he asked one of his own, 'So—why are you vulnerable, Philippa? And about what, or whom?'

'Oh—this is getting too complicated,' she said crossly. 'I was enjoying the peace and tranquillity of the lakeside, the colours of nature are so restful. Perhaps I could bring your father down here tomorrow. It might do him some good.'

'It's quite a way to push his chair,' he considered for a moment. 'We'll think of something.' He hesitated. 'Would you like to see inside my rather primitive log cabin while you're here?'

'I'd love to.'

'Come along then.'

It all seemed so unreal, walking with him under the trees in the quiet of the afternoon. They could be the only two people left in the world, she mused, wondering how long she could go on pretending they were, and a little smile played around her mouth which Harley saw but didn't comment on. Perhaps he had a very good idea what motivated it for he slipped his hand under her bare arm to guide her around a deceptively innocent pile of earth.

'Red ants. Be careful of them—they have a habit of burrowing into one's skin and sometimes it even necessitates minor surgery.'

'I wouldn't have known . . .' her voice was a little uneven because of his touch and the resultant quick-fire sensations.

'Yes. So always cover your head if you're under trees when it's raining or has been, Philippa. They drop on you from above and it's no joke getting rid of them.'

'I'll remember that. Oh—how lovely it looks standing there with the sun on the roof.' She had stopped to look at his log-built cabin interestedly. 'I didn't realise the craftmanship which goes into the building of one of these. Every log cut to size and put on top of each other—and all the same thickness—the criss-crossed corners and those through them for support.'

'And room division. Yes—it's solid enough and has probably seen well over a hundred winters.' The door was standing open. 'Come on inside. What do you think? I've had this fireplace rebuilt with some of the stone from the foothills and put in new windows. No double glazing when this cabin was put up. Oh—I've updated the bathroom with a shower. Oh yes—and replaced one or two roof beams. I'm at the décor stage now and I will need some help there.' He was watching her all the time.

'Is it to be a retreat or are you—planning to live here?'

What she really meant was, was he doing it for Rachel and himself.

'Just somewhere of my own where I can unwind when I feel the need; and fish—most relaxing that. Recharges one.'

'I like the feel of it,' she said simply as she looked around at the wood-lined walls.

'Good. I've already decided on a few prints I happen to like living with and the low tables and chairs are being craftsman-made by a master carpenter Rachel's father put me on to. So, I hope to complete it before fall.'

'It will be lovely. You see, I like natural materials so I feel in tune. I have a thing about imitations—I expect I'm a snob at heart.'

He had come close behind her—she felt his hands on her shoulders kneading gently the muscles in front of them. 'Unwind—Philippa . . .' he begged. 'You're tied up in knots—relax, my love.'

All her resistance slipped away as she turned into his arms. He gave a little muffled groan and bent his head to kiss her, feeling her mouth soft and responsive beneath his. Her arms crept up around his neck, her fingers moving gently through the dark hair which grew there, as she had wanted to do so many times before.

He moulded her close to his body, his hand on the small of her back and at once his kiss deepened, hungrily, urgently now, until they drew apart, breathless and flushed, and she knew he was questioning her wordlessly.

She looked up tremulously then into the dark passionate eyes, her own no longer cornflower but deepened disturbingly, to the man who wanted to make love to her right now, so desperately.

'God—I want you . . .' he burst out, while his arms tightened around her again.

Philippa hid her flushed face against his shoulder, her lips moving lightly against his neck, firing him more than she knew. 'I—want . . .' she began shyly; the rest of her words dying in her throat.

They both heard the hum of an outboard motor through the open door and the hiss as it was abruptly switched off.

With an irritated groan Harley put her gently away and, running a hand over his ruffled hair, strode to the window. But Philippa knew already whose feet were crunching over the pebbles and would soon reach the door.

'Of all the times to choose,' Harley muttered angrily, throwing her a frustrated look.

'Perhaps—it was the right time,' Philippa said quietly as she pushed her hair back from her forehead, tucking in her blouse with unsteady fingers. Even her legs were trembling so she waited on the same spot, her arms clasped lightly across her chest, as Rachel stood in the doorway.

'Hi . . .' she scrutinised them both with narrowed eyes. 'What goes on?' But now she was looking at Harley. 'Is this a private session or can anyone join in?'

'You already have,' he said drily, moving away from the window. 'So what brought you over, Rachel? You were going out with your mother.'

'Oh—I changed my mind.'

You knew I was here, Philippa decided, noticing how the other girl's eyes had gone straight to the divan the moment she came through the door. It stood along one wall and was covered with an exquisitely hand-made rug of interwoven colours, the scatter cushions matching.

Glancing now at Harley's face which only just controlled a smouldering anger, she said lightly, 'I must go. I don't want to be away too long.'

'Since that's what you're supposed to be here for,' Rachel said with a strong hint of sarcasm.

Harley too ignored that remark, coming across to Philippa's side. 'Would you like me to walk back with you?'

'Oh—no,' she assured him, moving towards the door. 'I expect you'll be up later.'

He nodded, holding the door for her.

'Mother said to remind you that we're eating at eight,' Rachel put in quickly, going to put a possessive hand on his arm. 'It's going to be quite a party.'

Philippa went quickly out into the golden sunshine of the afternoon, unable now to hear Harley's deeper tones which followed her as he replied to Rachel's remark.

She took the path through the trees and now it no longer mattered if the angry tears burned her eyes. Why had she fallen under the spell of his male magnetism yet again, when she knew he was simply stringing her along the way Nick had done? Were all men that devious?

It no longer mattered when the tears burned her eyes, even when something plopped on to her bare arm as she brushed them away. But it clung to the tender skin and, half angrily, she removed the small red insect about which he had warned her, rubbing at the sting it left behind.

She wouldn't give her thoughts house-room—not

those kind which beat into her brain with insistence because they could be true. Thoughts of Harley and Rachel alone in the cabin; maybe she was in his arms now, just as she had been. Rachel had no inhibitions, she guessed rightly, so what man would pass up the opportunity to satisfy his male ego? He was only human, after all. And he and Rachel . . .

No. I won't think that. Harley couldn't—not after the way he had wanted to love her just now, desperately, the magic of their coming together not just purely physical. There had been so much more of gentle awareness before the passion mounted and engulfed them both. If Rachel hadn't come—she could not have resisted him; her need as great as his. But he couldn't feel that way about Rachel too. There had been the wonder and quality of discovering something together which lifted them above everything but each other in that precious moment in time.

Yet what did she know of his personal life? Even at the hospital? He wasn't immune to women's company and chose them carefully. Because of his arrogant nature he was strongly self-disciplined too. Maybe there was just Rachel in his life seriously—which left her as another one of his flirtations—satisfying his need to make any woman fall for him, after which he lost interest. Well— she had been warned. Enough was enough. From now on Rachel need feel no anxiety on her behalf.

But as she climbed the green pastures towards the house, her new resolve was fading. That kiss had been the most devastating of her life. The joy in his arms as they closed round her, just what her body craved. He wasn't pretending, she was sure of that now. And what might have happened if Rachel hadn't shown up, she dared not think. It was so beautiful—until she came to spoil it. Of course, she knew I was there, she saw me from across the lake—she was thinking clearly now. Saw Harley come and join her too, watched them go back to the lodge together. It hadn't taken her long to hop in the boat and skim across the smooth stretch of water either. What had she expected to find? she wondered miserably, noticing the river flowing gently down to the creek.

She's jealous and possessive. The thought spun to certainty as she reached the veranda steps. A lovely afternoon spoiled utterly by a dark-haired girl who obviously had more priority in Harley's life than she. Another disappointment—they were spending the evening together. Well—she couldn't expect him to stay home with only her for company, and Brett, of course. Because once his father was settled for the night, it would be quiet, why should he pass up a party? It was only natural he should want to see the friends he had grown up with, she argued, against the overwhelming power he had now over her deeper senses, which now easily ruled her more sensible thinking.

Brett was waiting for her, Clyde having gone into the house.

'He dozed most of the afternoon,' he explained, 'then he wanted to go to his room.'

'Is he all right?' she asked anxiously.

'I guess so. He gets nervous when you're not around though. But he's presently talking to one of his friends on the phone. It seems he was invited to a party on the other side of the lake tonight and the invitation never got answered.'

'Oh . . . I expect he's missing out because at the hospital there is always someone qualified within call, and not here. He feels bereft. He is afraid of having another coronary; that's really the problem.'

'And—can he?'

'Yes,' she said quietly. 'Which is what we are all trying to avoid. But he is, as I expect Harley has told you, in a rather fragile situation.'

'It could happen any time. That's what you really mean, isn't it?'

'If something precipitates it—yes. But he's so much happier here that we're hoping his heart muscles will improve a little.'

'Sure,' he agreed positively. 'Let's just keep our fingers crossed for him. By the way, Aileen's back and she's made some tea.'

'That sounds very much like home . . .' she said gratefully. 'Do you want some?'

'Not for me. I'm a coffee man. But Father does—as you know.'

'Right. I'll take it along to him.'

Aileen poured tea, putting two cups on the tray for her to take along to her patient's room.

'Where is Maura? I haven't seen her today?' Philippa enquired.

'Playing with Johnnie, Larry's boy. They brought back a new game from the store. And . . . .' she confided, 'I got myself a dress—off the peg, of course, but it came out from Prince George only this week. I'll show you later. Tell me what you think. It's a bit—well, you know—not quite like me. I just felt I should break out a little. Now I'm not sure . . .'

'Show me later . . .' Philippa told her smilingly. 'I'm sure it's very nice.'

'More than that—it's sort of exciting.'

'Then it has to be good for you—there's nothing better for a tonic than a new dress,' she said positively.

Clyde was delighted and relieved to see her and it showed. 'I'm glad you're back,' he said simply.

'I needn't have gone,' she reminded him gently. 'You insisted. I won't leave you again.'

'I missed you, I guess. Did you see Harley anywhere?' He was waiting for an answer.

She nodded, turning her back; remembering Harley's kiss that she was never going to forget. 'Yes. He showed me his cabin. He really loves that place, doesn't he?'

'Always did. When he was a little boy, we knew where to find him if he was missing and in those days it was just a bunk-house for the guys up here for a weekend's fishing.'

'Rachel came over in her boat.'

'Did she now? But Harley's going over there tonight for a family celebration. Ruby wedding or whatever. Her parents are making a big thing of it. I've got an invitation somewhere which I forgot about. Harley can represent the De Winton group. Brett wasn't asked.'

'Why, I wonder?' she asked curiously.

'They have their reasons, no doubt. It's a long story. Greta and Louise, Rachel's mother, used to visit each other and the kids played together since they were knee-high.'

And still are, she mused, as she brought water for his tablets.

'I'll change for dinner,' he said unexpectedly. 'My blue silk shirt and tuxedo—and there are some black pants in there somewhere. Maybe I can get into them now. We'll have a party of our own—you and Brett and me; and tell Aileen she is to eat with us—when Maura is asleep.'

'I'll tell her this very minute.'

Clyde was in a strangely preoccupied mood tonight, she decided, as she went into the corridor with the tray of empty cups and collided with Harley who was about to come into the room.

His arms, used to steady them both, lost no time in holding her elbows, drawing her towards him. But with the tray between, it was easy to convince him that she wanted none of it, pushing him away with her free hand.

'Oh—we're off on that tangent again, are we?' he commented drily. 'When will you see other than what is under your nose, Philippa? You're not a child, for heaven's sake. Or—perhaps you are—in some things.' And shaking his head resignedly, he walked past her into his father's room.

In the kitchen she found Aileen preparing part of that night's meal.

'Fresh salmon?'

'One of the boss's favourites,' she confided, 'and only caught last night.'

'You mean—caught here.'

'Yes. Harley brought it back with him. And I thought lemon meringue to follow. And his special cheese.'

'We'll have to watch that, cholesterol-wise. But he sent me to insist that you join us tonight. He's changing specially. So you can wear your new dress.'

Aileen's eyes lit up—but only for a moment before she looked shyly down at the fish she was preparing. Then she said lightly, 'We shall be four then . . .' and now her eyes were darkly mysterious beneath the finely arched brows as she turned to lift a huge fish kettle down from a shelf and a little smile teased the corner of her well shaped mouth and, for the first time, Philippa realised that she could be a very attractive lady. Why then did she choose to make so little of herself, playing down her best assets?

Harley came along to the bathroom. She heard the water running and went back to her patient.

'You're not wearing uniform tonight,' he insisted. 'So go change before I want you here to help me.'

'You're the boss,' she said laughingly.

'And—don't anyone forget it . . .' he finished for her. So she left him gazing out across the valley between the foothills where some of his herd of beef cattle chewed away endlessly, and Clyde thought it the most lovely scene in his world.

Changing into a soft pale yellow cotton dress, its full skirt hugging her small waist, its low round neck and elbow-length sleeves a foil for the creamy skin which seldom saw enough sun to tan, she felt and looked good. She was about to go back to Mr De Winton but Harley opened his door, going along to the bathroom again with his towel over his arm. And that ridiculous towelling robe. The last thing she wanted was to meet him again wearing that, which was why she stood back and waited until he closed the bathroom door.

But his long legs, darkly covered with hair, did something to her equilibrium and she stood against her door-post breathing rather unevenly. At least she wouldn't have to think too much about him this evening and would be able to relax over their meal without feeling his eyes on her and knowing she dared not look up and meet them head on.

He appeared wearing his dinner suit, just as his father was ready to be wheeled along to the lounge.

His eyebrows went up in surprise at the sight of Clyde, resplendently immaculate in his silk shirt, and Philippa, looking lovelier than he had ever seen her, standing with her hand on his wheelchair in the glow of the blazing colours of a fiery sunset which streamed in through the open windows.

'Somebody's birthday?' he asked jokingly. 'I think I should have stayed over here. You're not having that salmon I caught are you, as well?'

'We are—my boy . . .' Clyde told him chuckling, his

silver hair brushed to one side. 'Philippa and I are going to a party, aren't we, honey?'

'We're not going anywhere until you've calmed down a little,' she insisted, throwing a pleading look to Harley.

But he merely said, 'Enjoy your evening, Dad. Glad you feel good, but don't overdo it.'

'I won't, Harley. Have a good time yourself with Rachel.'

'Thanks,' he said shortly, going ahead of them and out through the huge door into the summer evening, slamming the mesh inner door behind him.

'What's eating him, I wonder?' Clyde commented— and Philippa thought about that too.

CHAPTER TEN

BRETT brought drinks out on to the veranda, rising to the occasion when he saw that Philippa and his father had changed specially. He too looked very different tonight in his light pants and cream silk shirt with mother of pearl snap buttons on cuffs and shirt front—true cowboy style.

Aileen was putting Maura to bed but supper time was flexible tonight as she was serving the salmon cold with, Philippa noticed, some quite exotic looking salads.

The mosquitoes buzzed noisily but Philippa was adept at keeping them at bay now and the three of them sat quite comfortably listening to the birds, their night songs from the river suspended in the air. Mist hovered like an ethereal veil between the silent hills, catching the dying rays of the scarlet and orange sunset. Each was immersed in their own thoughts while they sipped Martinis and didn't hear Aileen until she said that supper was ready in her quiet voice.

Brett got to his feet slowly, his large body unwinding from the low chair, a look of incredulity appearing on his weathered face as he saw the transformation she had wrought.

Philippa jumped up full of admiration for the effort Aileen had made so successfully. Her brown hair, which had been previously mousy and subdued, was softer, fuller, a burnished shine to it now—and she had used make-up carefully, but effectively, her lipstick matching her nails. And Philippa guessed the deep pink dress with its frill at the neck and elbows and softly gathered skirt was quite different from her usual plain tops and skirts.

Her dark brown eyes were looking to Philippa for some confirmation, she gave her an immediate conspiratorial wink. Which only she saw.

Brett was certainly impressed and when he brought her drink he made no attempt to hide it. Which Philippa suspected was what Aileen had hoped for.

Clyde just raised his glass appreciatively. 'To the ladies—God bless 'em . . .' he said gallantly.

It was a perfect meal and Philippa tired hard not to let her thoughts stray across the lake to where Harley was no doubt enjoying himself with Rachel. Brett seemed in high spirits and she was discovering another hidden side to this quiet man whom she would have labelled the strong, silent type. Until this evening. He was rather an enigma—sometimes she saw traces of Clyde—but as he was adopted she ruled this out. Harley too—except that his eyes were brown and Clyde's grey-green—but only if you looked hard. They were usually half-closed.

She insisted on helping Aileen take out the dishes afterwards.

'Well, perhaps just this once,' the housekeeper said apologetically, 'but I'm not doing them tonight while I'm wearing this dress.'

'You look really good in it.'

'I feel good. I think that's the right word—kind of confident. But I'll never look like you do—even in your uniform dress you have—what is called flair, I think. And you're young too . . .'

'Well—thank you.'

'I think I should check Maura—if you'll keep an eye on the coffee. She's a bit snuffly tonight. I hope it isn't a summer cold. She seems to get them quite often.'

'Yes, of course. Is that the tray? I'll put out the cups and things.'

Aileen soon returned, saying that Maura was asleep. 'But I won't stay away for too long. She sounds a bit chesty tonight.'

'Mr De Winton won't be late either.'

'It's nice having you here,' Aileen told her shyly as she switched off the kitchen light behind them because, she explained, 'we have to generate our own electricity up here, so we don't waste it. But I wish it was for another reason that you came . . .' she ended wistfully as they crossed the hall to the lounge.

'So do I . . .' Philippa said fervently, as they went in to join the men.

Brett had put on a record so that soft music formed the background, along with the soft lighting. They sat drinking coffee in a restful, unhurried way, not needing to talk.

Philippa's keen eyes noticed when Clyde started to move restlessly, his leg especially, as he tried to get comfortable and failed. His fingers too began drumming the arm of his chair, then his knee.

'Are you all right?' she leaned to ask him quietly.

'No—I guess not. Got one hell of a pain in this leg. Had it all day.'

'You should have told me,' she said reproachfully.

'Thought it might go away—but it doesn't look that way. Damned nuisance. I'd better turn in.'

'Do you want a hand?' Brett asked, getting to this feet at once. But Clyde waved him away, allowing only Philippa to help him into his wheelchair again.

'Don't need you, Brett—except to open the door. You look after Aileen. I'm sorry to mess things up.'

'You haven't—it's been great,' Brett told him firmly, and Philippa threw him a grateful glance, for reassurance was everything to his father just now.

Clyde was in a good deal of pain until she finally

got him into bed with his leg resting on a pillow and had administered the necessary tablets ordered by Dr Gurnett, if such a complication occurred. And venous thrombosis was a complication. His pulse rhythm was irregular too but she could do nothing more except hope that this thrombosis would resolve itself and no further one or more would erupt elsewhere. She decided to wait up for Harley and let him call Dr Gurnett if he thought it necessary. It was the weekend and he would have left the hospital.

So she sat quietly in the armchair until he slept and then went through to the lounge.

Brett was watching television, a black and white movie, but he got up to switch off when she appeared.

'Don't—I'm not staying. What a voice that girl has—Deanna Durban, isn't it? Why do those oldies seem to have more romance than some of the current ones, I wonder?'

'Perhaps it's the long, floating dresses and tuxedos. We've become so casual about clothes these days—it's a bind to dress up. I confess to being hooked on those kind of films.'

'Well . . .' she said, 'you give an impression of being anything but romantic. Perhaps all men have a streak in them somewhere.' She was remembering Harley's gentle touch just before he kissed her that first time in the apartment. Then she became professional.

'But I didn't come to interrupt you to talk about romance, Brett. It's about your father's leg. I'll stay up with him until Harley gets back, I think. I don't want this thrombosis moving around too much. It's quite a blockage. Neither do I want to start fomentations, unless he advises it.'

'Dangerous?' he asked quietly.

'It could be, yes.'

'Shall I call Harley?'

'I don't like to do that. After all, I should have to cope if he was at Prince George. I'll see how it goes.'

'I just hope he does come back tonight, that's all.'

'I hadn't thought . . . Does he come across the lake after dark?'

'Not usually. He drove his car anyway.'

'I'll go back then.'

'Call me, if you're worried. I mean that.'

'I will. Where will you be? I mean—I don't know which is your room.'

'At the end of the corridor.' She saw the glimmer of an amused smile and realised that anyone listening could misconstrue their conversation. It was, after all, a leading question.

'Goodnight, Brett . . .'

''Night . . .' he said, abruptly for him.

She tried to read but words lost their meaning so she got up, staring out into the blackness of the lonely night. What was he doing? Dancing? Having a good time with his friends? It was, after all, his social scene and he grew up with these people, lived here until medical school and university. So, did he still feel he fitted in with them now? Or had hospital life, and death, changed his attitude to the people and things that mattered as a boy?

If only she could pack her bags and leave right now. Leave him to the girl he intended to marry sometime. Part of his world here. Perhaps Rachel didn't want to go to Prince George and live. Well—she couldn't have it both ways.

What if she hadn't come to the cabin today?

Harley must have known how much she wanted him to make love to her. She had almost thrown every other thought but that out of her mind. And if he had, she wouldn't be able just to walk away from him and out of his life as she soon must. But neither could she share him with Rachel who would try every ruse in her power to hang on to him.

How could she, with her fair, fresh face which was nothing out of the ordinary, compete with Rachel's arresting beauty and a passion beneath the surface which seemed to vibrate smoulderingly, just waiting to ignite. Did Harley really think he could play around with two women? One for weekdays—and another for more glamorous weekends?

She was back to square one and despising her own thoughts. Even with Nick, painful as it had been, she hadn't felt this burning jealousy of her rival. It had been her ego then. I wish I could just take off and go back to Edmonton, or even the UK and home, she thought. What on earth am I doing up here in the backwoods anyway? She knew the answer. Clyde needed to have her around. More than that, he trusted her to see him through. And she would, no matter what.

His pulse, though still ragged, hadn't worsened and although his breathing was noisy, he slept deeply.

Her watch hands pointed to one-thirty and she was debating whether to undress and go to bed, or make some coffee and wait for Harley, when she heard a door open and someone come running along the corridor.

'Aileen—what is it?'

'Maura—please come—she can't breathe—I think she's choking.'

Clyde hadn't stirred. The nurse in her wasted no more time and she didn't need to ask any questions. The raucous wheezing coming from their room told its own tale.

'Has she had asthma attacks before?'

'Nothing like this. I didn't know what to do.'

'Don't panic, Aileen. She's probably very frightened and needs reassuring.'

One look was enough. The child was struggling with every breath; able to breathe in but not out again, though she had fixed her shoulder girdle to make it easier herself. She was also congested in her face—her eyes like saucers.

Sitting on the bed, not attempting to get too close to her, knowing she needed all the air possible, Philippa said quietly, 'Don't be frightened, Maura—it will soon pass. Mummy is going to get lots of steam going in the room. That will help.'

She fetched two more supportive pillows, noticing the child's stomach rising and falling rapidly as she fought for breath.

Aileen already had a kettle plugged in and Philippa turned on the hot water tap in the basin. Fortunately it was very hot indeed. The air soon dampened but it was some time before the alarming wheezing sound eased.

Aileen was as frightened as her child. 'What she really needs is an antispasmodic,' Philippa whispered. 'I expect her blocked nasal sinuses precipitated this attack—I don't want to give her anything unless it's ordered by a doctor. You'll have to get an appointment at the hospital and have her checked for allergies. Something sparks it off and she probably has some infection as well. Ah— that's getting a little easier.'

But a fit of coughing started the wheezing up again and as Harley came into the hall, having already seen that lights were on, he heard and recognised the stertorous rasping sounds and came straight through the corridor, seeing Philippa there already.

'What have you given her?'

'Nothing yet. I do have adrenalin.'

'Good. 1000 solution—0–2—should do it. Switch off

the steam kettle now, Aileen. She'll do. And make some good strong black coffee, will you?'

Quickly checking Clyde, Philippa went back to where Harley was trying to distract Maura's attention from herself by telling her about another child who had asthma too. 'He's the best swimmer I know, so it needn't stop you doing things.'

She brought the hypodermic in a kidney dish.

'You had better do it,' he said in a low voice and so she reassured the terrified child, still heaving with each breath.

'Just one little prick, darling—and you'll soon feel much better. Aren't you lucky having a real doctor and nurse here on the spot to shoo your asthma away?'

It was over before she had finished talking and gradually the attack subsided and Maura fell into an exhausted sleep.

In the kitchen Brett, bare to the waist, had pulled on pants over his pyjama bottoms. He too had heard the child's raucous breathing and the four adults sat around the table drinking coffee and now it was Aileen who needed some back-up, beginning to tremble in the aftermath of a frightening experience.

'Get her some brandy, Brett . . .' said Harley. Then he went on to explain what she must do on Monday about getting more advice.

'I'll give you a letter for Dr Beard. He's the paediatric man at the hospital. I expect they'll take tests. She has a slight infection right now and she may need antibiotics. But—don't wrap her in cottonwool , Aileen, and try not to let her see that you're just as scared as she is. Just be as normal as possible if another attack occurs. There are several ways to prevent that happening, so get some advice.'

'I will,' she said gratefully.

Brett too said, 'Thanks . . .' nodding as he listened to his brother, as if it was his responsibility too.

'How is Dad now?' he asked and now all eyes were on Philippa. She pushed her hair back from eyes which threatened to close any minute.

'He's sleeping,' she said wearily.

'Something wrong there too?' Harley got up immediately. 'Why didn't you call me?'

'We decided that there wasn't much you could do,' she retorted. 'He has a venous thrombo, I think.'

'So—you haven't been to bed?'

She shook her head. 'No—I was waiting for you.'

'Oh—God . . .' he said irritably as she followed him along the corridor explaining what she had done, leaving Brett and Aileen still talking in the kitchen.

Harley decided there was no point in disturbing his father.

'He seems comfortable enough. You get some sleep, Philippa. I'll see him as soon as he wakes up. Goodnight.'

'Goodnight to you,' she murmured under her breath and could easily have burst into tears which might have released the pent-up emotion which he evoked.

But nature knew best and she remembered nothing more after her head touched the pillow.

It was Harley who turned restlessly and then lay staring up at the ceiling. He could so easily have come home earlier. Why the hell hadn't he? Philippa was an experienced nurse obviously but was the strain going to prove too much? Looking after his father out here without immediate medical facilities. Had they, in trying to placate Clyde in his longing to come home, put rather too much responsibility on to his young nurse's shoulders? Good nursing didn't rule out the emotional factor of involvement. He had seen the moisture gather in her eyes to be quickly blinked away. Maybe he should have a word with Brett to keep an eye on things as they developed.

Rachel arrived next morning just as Clyde was ranting about the Sunday papers.

'Don't they have to be collected?' Philippa reminded him gently.

'Well—there are enough people around the place surely. Where's Brett?'

'He's busy. Harley has gone for them.' She dared not tell him that Brett and three of the ranch hands had ridden out to the foothills to rescue one of the beef herd which had fallen into a gulley.

And also only half her mind was on her patient as she crossed to the window hearing Rachel's voice shouting to one of the boys leading a horse over to the corral.

'Where the hell is everybody?' she asked, running down the veranda steps.

'I'll go and see what she wants,' Philippa said. 'I expect Aileen is in with Maura after her traumatic night.'

'Harley—that's who she wants . . .' Clyde said dourly. 'Go and keep her away from this room. She's the last person I want to see this morning.'

Philippa met her as she was striding through the bedroom corridor.

'Hi. Where's everyone?'

'Harley has gone for the papers. Brett is out on the ranges.'

'I'll wait.' She eyed the nurse warily. 'I suppose you wish you were going back with him today?'

'Why should I?' Philippa responded coolly. 'I'm here to nurse Mr De Winton.'

'So I've been told. For how long?'

'I can't answer that. Would you like some coffee? Aileen's busy . . .'

'I'll wait. And I'm quite able to help myself. I am almost one of the family. Perhaps you didn't know that, Nurse Croft.'

'I suppose you mean that you're hoping to marry Dr De Winton sometime.'

'Of course. Soon, I expect.'

'I—didn't know you were engaged.'

'Who bothers with engagements these days. It's just a question of finalising our plans and deciding where we'll live.'

'I see.'

Her next words were the final straw. 'And perhaps, while we are alone I should warn you, I won't stand for any competition, Nurse Croft, if you have any ideas in that direction.'

'You flatter me,' Philippa retorted. 'I wouldn't attempt to take him away from you if I wanted to, which I don't. But if you're to marry him, shouldn't you try trusting him a bit more?'

'I saw you yesterday . . .' Rachel hissed. 'Do you think I don't know what was going on?'

'Then you don't need me to tell you, do you?' Philippa said sweetly, leaving her standing in the kitchen.

Harley's car wheels crunched on the gravel as she went back to Clyde's room. When he came with the papers she didn't look at him.

Rachel stayed to lunch. Roast beef and all the accompaniments. It reminded her of Sundays at home when her mother cooked the traditional lunch of beef and Yorkshire pudding in the heart of Cornwall.

Clyde was still resting his inflamed leg so as Philippa preferred to have hers in the kitchen with Aileen and Maura, pale but with her asthma resolved, the two men and Rachel had theirs in the dining-room.

Later, when Rachel went out to her red car, her voice came through Clyde's open window where Philippa was sitting quietly.

'You are coming next weekend, aren't you darling?'

'If it's at all possible.'

'It was good last night, wasn't it?'

'It was a good party—yes,' Harley said carefully.

'I—didn't mean that and you know it. You devil . . .' her tone was provocative.

'Next week then,' Harley said quickly. 'Now—I have to get my things together and start back.'

Philippa sighed deeply, feeling a painful tugging at her heart-strings. Who ever said there was no such thing as heartache? Well—she knew how things really were between those two now. She just wished Harley could have been more open about it, that's all.

Soon afterwards he came to say goodbye to his father. He was already the doctor figure again, in Philippa's mind; authoritative—private—and unsmiling.

'I'll see you on Friday, if all goes well—take it slowly. You're in excellent hands.'

'I knew that before you did, Harley.'

Clyde was sorry to see him go, feeling a little of his security slipping away with him, although he was grateful for Philippa's supportive nursing because, but for her, he would still be in those four pale blue walls at the hospital.

Rachel came across the lake during the week with a basket of nectarines from her father's hothouse. But Clyde didn't want to see her.

'Now—if it was her mother . . .' he said jokingly. 'She might be very good for me—but perhaps not.'

So Philippa went to make excuses.

'I'm afraid he isn't feeling too well.'

'What does that mean?' Rachel glared back at her, pulling off her sunglasses with an angry gesture.

'That he is rather poorly. His leg is painful.'

'Has he heard from Harley?'

'Oh, yes. Haven't you? He called last night to say that Dr Gurnett is coming with him on Friday and staying the night.'

'What on earth for?'

'As Dr De Winton's guest, I presume.'

She had left then but later, when Clyde asked the same question, why Dr Gurnett thought it necessary to come all that way just to see him, she explained more fully.

'On Saturday he is going on down to Vancouver for a seminar and it seemed a good idea to break his journey and stop over here for one night. I expect Harley wants to show off the ranch and his lodge and he'll have a look at you at the same time.'

Clyde grunted. 'Makes sense . . .'

'Of course it does.'

She would also have his opinion too. Clyde was showing signs of other complications now and some oedema which could necessitate a further change in his medication. Her job was becoming more difficult and not less as they had hoped.

She quietly watched him for a time as he slept, glad that Harley would be here tonight.

Rachel as well, she supposed, after Dr Gurnett had gone. As his future wife she had some precedence. There had to be some way she could show Harley that she knew this to be true now. It had to be. Rachel wouldn't dare lie about something like that. Besides—her family and friends were part of his background too. All perfectly natural, except where had she fitted in? Part-time nurse? Except as a diversion.

Maybe it was because of his guest that Harley failed to see that Philippa's quiet manner was any different. Clyde was given tests which kept her busy and, as far as possible, a thorough going over. It was comforting to have the two doctors in the house that night for, privately, she was very worried about her patient and wished, in an emergency, he could be got into hospital more quickly.

Next morning, before he left, Dr Gurnett put her completely in the picture and she knew there was no way she could relinquish her job yet.

'His condition is deteriorating, as you must have seen for yourself,' he told her. 'Ideally—he should come back into hospital but that would probably kill him. I've changed his tablets, as you'll see from this—but I've brought a supply of these new anti-coagulants. We can but try them. I shall alert them at Quesnel—just in case they're needed but it's quite a way to come. Dr De Winton will leave you a number to call. Can you cope, Nurse?'

He looked at her over the top of his gold-rimmed glasses.

Philippa didn't hesitate. 'Yes, Dr Gurnett.'

Harley did know very well that she was avoiding him. It piqued him and once Dr Gurnett's powerful car had disappeared around the bend of the river he lost no time in seeking her out.

'Can I have a word?' he asked quietly, thinking that Clyde was dozing. She had been putting his folded clean things in the closet.

'Is it important?'

'*I* think so . . .'

But Clyde's voice from his pillows shattered any hopes he might have had.

'Harley—how much longer do I have to keep this

darned leg up? And what did that specialist have to say about my ticker?'

'You stay there until the inflammation resolves, Dad,' Harley spoke quietly, self-discipline taking over. 'He's quite happy about the rest of you but it might help if you'd let the ranch business go over your head for a time. I suppose that's asking the impossible.'

'You're darned right it is. I want to know what goes on out there. For two pins I'd get outside and see that some of that hay gets brought in. This ranch wasn't built up taking free weekends . . .'

'Brett's out there now,' Harley told him patiently, 'and the boys. Don't you hear that thresher going?'

'Sure,' he said in a more chastened tone.

'Yes. Well, I'm having some furniture delivered so that's where I'll be.' He glanced at Philippa but she turned away. No doubt Rachel will be there with him, she thought disconsolately, deliberately torturing herself further as he turned on his heel and strode away, feeling almost as frustrated as she.

He didn't know that she stood at the window watching his lean figure in blue jeans and sweat-shirt walk purposefully across the grass, the back of his dark head all she recognised of the doctor image, white coat flying—which was a part of her habitat. This was his other image and this one belonged to Rachel.

CHAPTER ELEVEN

BRETT was in the kitchen when Philippa went along to prepare Clyde's tray for supper. He was still a bit dozy from the sedative effect of his new tablets.

'It's not quite ready,' Aileen told her.

'So . . .' Brett said with a grin on his good-looking face, 'why not come and have a Martini? I've just collected some ice and lemons.'

'What a lovely thought. I think I will,' Philippa said appreciatively, going out to the veranda with him.

And Harley, who had come around the house, saw them standing there against the background of creeper which grew up the fencing, saw too the look on Brett's face as she smiled up at him as he handed her her drink, completely alien to the closed-in look he was used to seeing on his adopted brother's face, and got quite the wrong impression. He hadn't yet noticed that recently, since the night when the child was ill, a new Brett had emerged from a somewhat toughened chrysalis and so far he hadn't looked back, nor did he intend to!

'I'd like a drink too,' he said icily, coming into focus and climbing the veranda steps slowly. 'Unless I'm intruding . . .' he ground out, positively glaring at Philippa, his brow furrowed the way it had been at the lake in Edmonton. 'I see you're changed already, Brett. Things are somewhat different around here, aren't they?'

'Bourbon?' Brett seemed very much in command of the situation and Philippa watched while Harley took the drink then turned to face her, still looking angry about something.

'I didn't know you would be back for supper,' she said thoughtfully.

'So where did you think I'd be? So . . . ?' he asked belligerently.

Had Rachel said something to upset him, she wondered. There was no smile there for her, no gentle teasing—had she fired shots of her making, turning him against her? Could it be her own coolness which he hadn't seemed to notice earlier?

Putting her glass down, no longer enjoying her drink, she said quietly, 'Excuse me—I expect my patient's supper is ready now.'

Both men watched her go, head held high on her lovely supple body, and neither spoke for a time.

'Aileen . . .' Philippa said as she picked up the tray, 'I'll eat in here with you if you don't mind. I can hear if Mr De Winton calls then.'

Later, Harley came along to say goodnight to his father. 'I'm going over the other side—but I'll be back around eleven, I expect.'

This was mainly for Philippa's benefit and some relief crept into her eyes. She even smiled tremulously into his deeply smouldering ones but he simply turned and left her staring at the open door.

She didn't go along to the lounge again but in the dusk of the summer evening, when Clyde was asleep, she walked around the ranch house, enjoying the sweet, fresh air blowing gently in from the mountains, uplifting her jaded spirits. Through the kitchen window she noticed that Brett and Aileen were close in conversation. She saw Brett reach to push a strand of hair from her forehead with a gentleness she had not associated with him—until now.

They had come out to sit on the veranda when she reached it.

Pleading a headache she said goodnight and that she was going to bed early—and knew they had no objection.

The thought of a cool shower was an extremely pleasant one, so slipping out of her dress and the minute panties and bra underneath, she let the jets run deliciously over her skin until she felt cool and refreshed.

Taking a nightie from the drawer, she stood poised, slipping it over her head, her tensions released as she moved her neck and waist in gentle exercises before slipping into bed and reaching for her book. All the time she was deliberately shutting Harley out of her mind.

Her door was half-open, so that she could hear if Clyde called during the night. When Harley returned just after eleven-thirty, her light was still on and her book had slid to the floor.

He stooped to pick it up—hoping the click of the switch as he turned off her light wouldn't waken her. She was so deeply asleep, her hair soft and tumbled on the pillow. He touched a strand before silently going out and across to his own room, his thoughts turbulent.

How could he have let her slip through his fingers like that, leaving the way clear for Brett to step in? A changed Brett—all spruced up—the signs all there of the way he was feeling since she had come to the ranch. Why hadn't he come out with his own feelings before this? Instead, he had been waiting, holding back, while she got the other guy in the UK out of her system. Women were the very devil. You never knew where you were with them.

Rachel couldn't accept it when he told her that he wasn't in love with her and there was no question of them ever getting married. She had known, though, for a long time. He had been open enough about that; with her parents too. But with Philippa—he could have made it. Too late now. But the thought of her as she had looked just now tortured him in the summer night as he twisted restlessly, while outside the mosquitoes crashed against the mesh across his window in musical droves; until he turned out his light.

Philippa surfaced through layers of sleep, wondering what had disturbed her. It was still dark outside and silent. Not even the sound of Clyde's snoring or tortured breathing broke the stillness. It was too quiet . . .

She flung back her sheet and reached for her cotton dressing-gown, going along to his room, her bare feet making no sound on the red carpet.

She knew at once—the room so ominously still. 'No— oh, no . . .' Her lips moved in a silent prayer as she felt for his pulse—knowing it would no longer throb beneath her fingers as she looked down at his craggy face.

Was Harley back? Yes—he must be because his door was closed and had been half-open when she went to bed. What time was it—that was important. Just ten past three. She ran to Harley's door, knocking and going straight in.

He was lying, half-covered with just a sheet, moon-light streaming in over his darkly-haired chest, his head to one side.

'Wake up—Harley—please—wake up . . .' Touching his bare shoulder—more urgently, 'Harley . . .'

He sat up at once. 'What is it? Who—Philippa—is it . . . ?'

'Your father . . .'

He was out of bed and reaching for his short robe, following her urgently back to the room next door.

Like her, he knew at once. 'Oh . . . God . . .' he groaned. 'Why didn't I check him last thing when I came in? He was okay—his breathing not at all bad then . . .'

'I know. I—wouldn't have gone to bed at all . . .'

'Don't blame yourself, Philippa. You couldn't have done anything. Just cardiac failure. It could happen at any time . . .' he said miserably. 'It's the best thing—for him . . . He couldn't stand being an invalid for the time he had left. Will you go and wake Brett? I'll—just stay here a moment. How did you know though?'

'Something woke me—I don't know if—he—tried to call me . . .'

He shook his head. 'You're not to think that way.' He saw her eyes fill with tears which she fought hard to control. Her hands too were trembling when he took them in his. 'Don't—believe me—it's best this way. Go and get Brett—and pour us three brandies. Stiff ones.'

The three of them sat in the lounge quietly reminiscing. 'I guess it's always a shock,' Brett said huskily, 'even when it's half-expected. I didn't know it was that close.'

'The damage to his heart was very extensive,' Harley divulged. 'Dr Gurnett said that it couldn't hold out much longer. I don't know what precipitated the final attack though.'

'He was angry and frustrated about everything,' Philippa spoke at last. 'This is what did it—and because I wasn't at hand with his pills . . .'

'You can't be sure of that,' Harley assured her. 'No one can. Someone will have to come out from the hospital though. I'll call them in an hour or so. Fortunately Dr Gurnett was picking up another consultant from there and left a letter for the resident cardiologist. We can't do any more tonight, except . . .'

'I know,' Philippa said softly. 'I shall do that myself.'

'I insist on giving a hand,' Harley said firmly. She had no strength to resist.

The whole ranch was plunged into sorrow for a loved and respected boss. Cars came and went and after a few days Clyde was buried beside his beloved Greta, as he had wished.

When everyone had gone, including Rachel, Harley announced that he would go back to Prince George. 'I have patients waiting for instant surgery and I can't do any more here.'

'I'd like to come with you,' Philippa's eyes were very blue, washed with secret tears for so many things. 'Back to the hospital. Or on to Edmonton.'

'If that's what you want I'm sure they will be glad to have you—but—why Edmonton?'

'That's where I'm registered, isn't it?'

'But . . .'

'But what?'

'Oh—nothing. Come back with me tomorrow by all means. The apartment is vacant. Stay there until you know what your plans are. I'm leaving around nine.'

Next morning saw them leave after the goodbyes had been said, Brett and Aileen watching the car drive away from the doorway. A soft rain was falling over the creek and Philippa looked back to the ranch house saying a silent goodbye to Clyde whom she missed very much. He had been a very special person to her, more than just a patient and there was a lump in her throat as she remembered.

Because she seemed disinclined to talk, Harley made no attempt to break into her reverie with small talk. But after a few miles he spoke.

'Has Brett talked to you, Philippa?'

'About what?'

'You know that Father left him the ranch . . . ?'

'No. Not to be shared between you?'

He shook his head. 'No. Dad and I discussed this. The

ranch is Brett's. He'll keep it on the way Dad would have wanted. He was—a wealthy man—and left me a considerable sum of money which I intend to use towards cancer research and cardiology. The lodge and acreage by the lake are mine anyway. I've all I need. Brett will have a heritage for his family. When he has one.'

'The ranch is his whole life,' she said sadly.

'Well—he's his father's son—did you know that?'

'No. But he was quite a bit like him. It—had crossed my mind. Did your . . .'

'My mother know? Yes. Brett guessed too. It was disclosed in the will. We will never know who his mother was. It's Dad's secret now. My mother was a very special person and my father quite a character.'

'I know.'

For a second only his hand rested over hers in her lap. Then, seeing her face he changed to lighter, topical subjects. But she didn't want to talk, wondering what barrier kept coming between them, something she only sensed because of her sensitivity where he was concerned. After that wonderful closeness at the lodge cabin he had shut off. Because of his impending marriage to Rachel probably. But he didn't give the impression of being over the moon about that either.

He saw her into the apartment at Prince George and left, going straight on to the hospital. After an hour of getting settled in Philippa lifted the phone and called the nursing officer's secretary and was asked to come over that afternoon. Which she wasted no time in doing.

'We're desperate for a charge nurse in the fracture ward on Orthopaedic,' Matron told her. 'What with vacations and tourists driving like crazy through the town. Could you come in tomorrow?'

Next day when Harley came up to the ward to reassess one of his elderly patients with a fragmented fracture of the left tibia, which he was going to have to reset, he stared disbelievingly at first at the girl bending over the bed, her hand gripped by a rather distraught patient, while she soothed her quietly.

What a girl. And here she was, on his ward. She looked up and saw him and he dared not believe that her eyes lit up like that—specially for him. Bringing with her the patient's notes she led him to the table and began to discuss the case.

'Being diabetic doesn't help . . .' he began.

She agreed.

'Do you like working on this floor?' he asked curiously when they were through.

'Oh, yes.' She felt absolutely in command, until he was leaving after going through the list with her, when he said teasingly in an undertone,

'That ridiculous cap, Philippa. It's worse than your own . . .'

'It—becomes my status.' And as her eyes danced a little for him he shook his head.

Why the hell hadn't he done something about the way he thought of her? Why let Brett fall in love with her too? With every hope that she would be the mother of his children sometime. He knew he couldn't just stay around and watch that happen. But what of his log cabin? So much had gone into making that a home for himself. And the creek and the lake—and his family roots. They—meant something.

Philippa had switched her feelings from one brother to the other very fast—hadn't she? Did she tell the truth when she said she hadn't known about the ranch being Brett's?

I don't know that, he groaned inwardly as he retraced his steps back along the corridor and went down in the elevator to his row of waiting patients.

During the next days he almost worked himself to a standstill, scrubbing for one emergency after another with his two registrars.

The theatre staff decided that he was trying to work his father's death out of his mind. But he disciplined himself enough not to contact Philippa off duty. He couldn't trust his will-power that far. Not just to grab her when they were alone and convince her that he loved her so desperately—she just had to feel it too.

Then on the next Friday evening, just as she was walking slowly out into the city traffic build-up, Harley's car stopped.

'Are you off duty?' He leaned across, opening the door for her to get in.

She nodded. 'Unexpectedly—yes. Why?'

She saw his casual shirt and slacks and had noticed his bag on the back seat.

'You're off this weekend then? Going to the ranch?' She didn't want him to think her too curious. But she had to know.

'Yes. Pity you aren't off too—I could have run you down as well.'

'But I am—Sister Jetson wants to take next weekend off instead of this—to go to a wedding somewhere, so I've swapped with her.'

'Come with me then . . .'

'I'd love to,' she said wistfully.

'Get your things and just come then. Brett wants to talk over a few things needing my signature. I'm certain he'll be delighted when I drive up with you.'

She puzzled over this. He went on—

'Aileen's small girl is struggling with her asthma again too. She keeps calling for you strangely—not even her mother. I'm glad I stopped. I—almost didn't.'

'Why ever not? I'm just glad you did. I wonder what

advice Aileen has been able to get over that child. And because her mother is so scared, quite naturally—it makes Maura worse. Have I got time to change?'

'I'll wait,' he said, smiling up at her when she got out.

It was like coming home. They had arrived in time for a late supper and today the journey didn't seem quite so long.

Philippa missed Clyde being there and she knew Harley did too. But they all knew the ranch had to go on without him.

Maura was much better. One of the medical team had come out by road that day and given her the drug Aminophylline as an emergency measure when the attack hadn't subsided after twenty-four hours, and shown Maura how to use the Ventolin inhaler.

'And stay away from the stables,' he had advised. 'It seems you're allergic to horse hair and things like straw and hay. We'll see how you go on . . .'

'I wanted you to come—so badly,' Maura told Philippa when she knew she was there. 'Where were you?'

'At the hospital looking after people with broken or dislocated bones—and they need me too . . .'

'So do I—God knows—how much . . .' Harley breathed under his breath, turning away from her lovely smile which sent his senses rocketing.

Philippa noticed that he made no attempt to contact Rachel and after supper on Saturday evening she went down to the lakeside, wondering if she dared go out on the lake by herself for a little while. It looked so peacefully still. She began to feel the peace of it seeping into her very soul as she threw back her head and just wandered on. Past the boathouse. Acting on impulse now she walked towards the clearing and the log cabin.

It looked lived-in somehow, the windows shining in

the last rays of the sun. There seemed to be no one around so she went closer, peering in the windows, curious to see the chairs and furnishings Harley had told her about. There were books on the shelves, lamps on low tables and rugs on the polished wood floor. It was finished now.

Without thinking, she turned the iron handle on the thick wooden door and pushed it slowly open. 'Is anyone there?'

Only silence. Would Harley think it an intrusion if she only stayed a short time? Would he even know? It was somehow a part of him. The home he wanted—his favourite things around him.

She stood there, her hand pressed to her mouth, looking around at the work he had put into it. The fireplace—laid ready with logs. Through the doorway a kitchen with wood fittings to match the beams across the roof. She felt a little like standing in a church. A little awed . . .

As she turned to go a shadow moved near the door. Harley had been leaning against the beam, watching her through narrowed eyes.

'Oh—I'm sorry. I'm trespassing aren't I?' she said shakily because now there was something very determined in the way he moved towards her. Slowly; while his eyes took in her silk shirt and the cream culottes she enjoyed wearing, her bare legs and flat sandals, then back to her face again.

'Yes . . .' he said unsteadily, as he reached her and lifted her chin with one finger. 'I think you are.' Then looking deep into her eyes, he murmured, even while she felt the tremor in his body as he bent his mouth almost to hers, 'I suggest you marry me and put that right. Because then it would be yours too . . .'

'Don't tease . . .' she begged, turning her mouth away

from his, but only slightly. 'I—can't bear it . . .'

'Oh—my darling—don't you know I want that more than anything else? Don't you know that I've been almost out of my mind thinking it was Brett? Until just now—when he told me that he's going to marry Aileen—as soon as it can be arranged.'

Her lips parted and now he quickly covered her mouth with his own.

'I love you . . .' he said huskily when at last the kiss had reduced them both to an intense need of each other. So that she couldn't not know how much he wanted to love her. Her own body was behaving instinctively towards his in a way she hadn't experienced before either, as she clung to him unashamedly.

It was then he kicked the door closed behind him and lifted her in his arms and carried her to the divan, putting her down gently on to its beautiful cover.

'You look wonderful with your hair spread like that all over the cushion,' he whispered. 'I—imagined you here like this.'

Then his deeply passionate kisses robbed her even of her own identity and she only knew that this was where she belonged as her arms held him close.

'I—love you so much . . .' he heard her murmur when his lips were away from hers for a moment.

'And I you—my darling. Are you happy?'

'Oh—so happy,' she murmured drowsily as the shadows deepened outside and even the trees seemed to be whispering in approval.

The lovely night stretched away until dawn; a night of discovery when Philippa knew that what she had thought to be real love between a man and woman had only been lukewarm pretence. Now she knew what it really meant to be in love. This oneness—in Harley's arms—beyond anything she had dreamed it could be.

'Won't they wonder—up at the house,' she whispered, stirring in his hold once more.

'I—shouldn't think so—they might even be glad we decided to stay here,' he murmured against her ear.

And after that they didn't even notice the rosy dawn in the sky. The start of a new day.

Take your holiday romance with you

STARFIRE – Celia Scott.
CHANCE MEETINGS – Vanessa James.
SAVAGE PAGAN – Helen Bianchin.
HARD TO GET – Carole Mortimer.

Price £4.40

Mills & Boon

THE ROSE OF ROMANCE

Doctor Nurse Romances

Amongst the intense emotional pressures of modern medical life, doctors and nurses often find romance. Read about their lives and loves in the other three Doctor Nurse titles available this month.

HEARTACHE IN HARLEY STREET
by Sonia Deane

Harley Street is a world apart, full of tragedy, apprehension, relief and happiness. Heartache too, Nurse Anita Fielding discovers when she comes to work for consultant gynaecologist Ross Wyndham, who is not only a brilliant surgeon but also a charming and attractive man.

A MODEL NURSE
by Sarah Franklin

'Love is an item that is not on my agenda – at least for another three years.'
Nurse Crystal O'Hara has her career mapped out, until Dr Craig Sands walks into her life and she finds that love has a way of ignoring things like agendas!

LOVE ME AGAIN
by Alexandra Scott

The whole hospital – at any rate, the feminine half of it – was agog with excitement over the new consultant, Andrew Steward. All, that was, except Eva Smith. But then no one else knew what she and Andrew had once been to each other. And Eva at any rate did not know how she could bear to be near him again, knowing that now she meant less than nothing to him . . .

Mills & Boon
the rose of romance

4 BOOKS FREE
Enjoy a Wonderful World of Romance...

Passionate and intriguing, sensual and exciting. A top quality selection of four Mills & Boon titles written by leading authors of Romantic fiction can be delivered direct to your door absolutely FREE!

Try these Four Free books as your introduction to Mills & Boon Reader Service. You can be among the thousands of women who enjoy six brand new Romances every month PLUS a whole range of special benefits.

- Personal membership card.
- Free monthly newsletter packed with recipes, competitions, exclusive book offers and a monthly guide to the stars.
- Plus extra bargain offers and big cash savings.

There is no commitment whatsoever, no hidden extra charges and your first parcel of four books is absolutely FREE!

Why not send for more details now? Simply complete and send the coupon to MILLS & BOON READER SERVICE, P.O. BOX 236, THORNTON ROAD, CROYDON, SURREY, CR9 3RU, ENGLAND. OR why not telephone us on 01-684 2141 and we will send you details about the Mills & Boon Reader Service Subscription Scheme — you'll soon be able to join us in a wonderful world of Romance.

Please note:— READERS IN SOUTH AFRICA write to Mills & Boon Ltd., Postbag X3010, Randburg 2125, S. Africa.

- -

Please send me details of the Mills & Boon Reader Service Subscription Scheme.

NAME (Mrs/Miss) _____ EP6

ADDRESS _____

_____

COUNTY/COUNTRY _____

POSTCODE _____

BLOCK LETTERS PLEASE